The Jailer's Son

Exile

S. A. Ferkey

Visit my website: http://www.saferkey.com
Email: saferkey@saferkey.com

Contemporary and Historical Fiction by S. A. Ferkey

Westerns:
The Jailer's Son Series
Book 1: The Legend Begins
Book 2: Where There's Will, There's A Way
Book 3: Exile
Book 4: No Patience

Action Adventure:
Steel Joe
Alaska Wilde

Contents

To Ma and Pa

Chapter 1

No End to Trouble

1889 Near the Colorado/Utah Territory Border

Something wasn't quite right. I heard it between the occasional patter of rain and distant rumble of thunder. I felt it too, like some old codger instead of the sixteen-year-old I was. Most of my aches n' pains were remnants of the beatings and such that I received at the hands of the traveling show. Right now they were tellin' me now that if I wasn't on my toes, I'd be getting another wound to take with me to my grave.

Hinto flashed me a look. It was so easy and natural that if I wasn't me, I'd believe it was just a glance in passing. But knowing him as I did, I was sure he was confirming my suspicions that something bad was brewing nearby.

I had an inkling it was another bounty hunter, but it truly could've been just about any fool thing – someone hearing a story about me, and seeing if they could get one up on me. Or maybe it was just a man trying to steal one of our horses. I'd encountered both, and more, in the year I'd been in exile.

There were times my skin would set to crawlin' late at night. And if Huàn would give me a low nicker or warning snort, I'd know my unease wasn't for naught.

I'd been away from the CB for close to a year, but there wasn't a day that I didn't think of everyone there and hope they were safe and well. And I thought about Patience, livin' at her grandparents' home, twice as often. I hoped she was still thinking about me, but I wasn't a fool. A girl so pretty would have a steady stream of suitors to choose from should she so desire.

It was probably normal for a wanted man like me to start feeling like things were never gonna work out when you had someone on your tail day in and day out.

Maybe it was thinking about it, or maybe it was intuition, but the hair on the back of my neck suddenly stood on end. On cue, Huàn nickered but I didn't give him one iota of attention.

"Gonna take a piss," I told Hinto as I started to get up. I could tell by the look in his eye, he knew exactly what I was gonna do.

We were sheltered by boulder on two sides, which was either good or bad, depending on where we happened to be if we got attacked. Still, it was better than being in the open.

The crumbling sandstone afforded us protection from the elements and also potshots. Animals would come say howdy once in a while, but we'd either shoo 'em away or have something for supper that we didn't have to go lookin' for.

The natural L shape of our cover was easy to take refuge in or get out of it in a hurry too. The slight overhang of the top of one of the boulders was almost like having a tent. And if someone happened to get a drop on us, we had a little surprise planned for him.

Cuh-lik.

I had no more than stood up, when I heard that sharp, yet slightly muffled sound. I heaved a mental sigh. I used to love hearing the sound of metal against metal when I was younger. Now I was starting to grow weary of it.

Pinpointing the sound while I moved as though I didn't hear it was going to be a bit tricky. I still hadn't fully recovered from the beatings I'd received at the hands of my

6

grandfather, Liling, and Chester when I'd been held captive in the traveling show. My agility wasn't what it once was, and I wasn't foolhardy enough to hope it would suddenly all come back in a rush.

I also knew whoever was getting a bead on me was gunning for me alone. It made me feel kinda sorry for Hinto. Here he was, at a time in his life when he should've been takin' it easy and not having to struggle. Instead, he was getting shot at, at least once a week just for riding with me.

Hinto never complained, though. He seemed comfortable with me, as if we'd been friends our whole lives. Or maybe he still felt responsible for me, even though I was a man now. Sometimes I wondered if he considered me a son that sorta got thrust on him, but then got accustomed to me.

Keh–

Two guns. This one sounded like a small pistol.

Huàn whinnied his warning as I dove to the ground, reaching for my Colt, as I scanned the rough, dusky horizon.

–lik! Ke-powow! Ke-powow ke-pooooow!

I hit the ground a little rougher than I wanted to, feeling boulder shrapnel from ricocheting bullets nick my face and neck on the way down. My hip protested the moment I made contact with the ground, mainly because I landed on a boot-sized chunk of rock I had planned on kicking out of the way after we set up camp. Now I'd mostly likely pay for my oversight with a nice bruise and a welt.

However, if I didn't find out who the shooters were in a hurry, a welt would be the least of my problems.

I twisted, righting myself as I thrust my trusty Cold into position. Hinto caught my eye for a fraction of a second. He already had an arrow out of his quiver and tight against his drawn bow. The old man was a quick one.

With a nod, he indicated that I should take the rear.

Zing! Ka-powow! Kuh-zing! Powowow!

Somebody had a lot of ammo to waste. That or they really wanted me dead.

Zing! was the noise I focused all my diminished powers of concentration on. It was close by. In the background, I heard Huàn buckin' and raising a vocal ruckus. He wasn't trying to break free; he was doin' what I'd trained him to do – create a distraction.

It was in the first moment of Huàn's pitchin' a fit that I caught an almost imperceptible movement a few yards away, where me and Hinto had been sitting. Someone thought they were gonna get the drop on me.

I knew there was at least one other man out there, but Hinto would keep his eyes peeled where mine weren't, so I focused on taking care of whoever was intent on finishing me off.

Cuh–

It was the fumbled sound of someone clumsily bringing back the hammer of an old firearm. I swung my Colt up toward the movement and thumbed my hammer back. I quickly released the trigger when I realized who was so intent on doin' me in.

A woman!

In the middle of a bolt of lightning zigzagging across the sky – chain lighting – I dove again. As I hit the earth, I tried to figure out how I could end this trouble with both of us still breathing in the end. I wasn't about to shoot a woman without knowing why she wanted me dead so bad.

Chuk! The bullet missed me by an inch. She was gonna kill me for sure if I stayed still, and I wasn't in the mood to roll around in the dirt and rocks all night tryin' to evade her bullets.

The accompanying clap of thunder came right on top of the gunshot.

"Stop yer shootin', lady!" I called up to her.

"Why should I?" she screeched back in a voice so loud, it almost sounded like she was speaking into an amplifying horn. She really didn't need to yell. I wasn't that far away. But maybe she wanted her partner to get a better shot at me.

"Do I even know you?" I asked. I purposely kept my voice little more than a whisper. That way she'd have to come closer to hear me. It would also give Hinto a better target if need be.

I kept my Colt out, but also grabbed a rock with my left hand – just in case. I could throw just as well with my left as I did with my right.

"You killed George!"

Which meant she'd been a part of the traveling show. I had to admit I was surprised by the sheer tenacity of the raggedy band of the show survivors.

They had dogged my heels for the first six months after me and Hinto headed away from the tattered remains of the show. Then nothing. I truly thought no one else was left, though I still had nightmares every once and while about Liling. They involved her in some evil capacity of power, or they had me watching her crawling off somewhere to die. When I was awake, I hoped it was the latter.

I heard the sound of running feet behind me, slow and heavy, like whoever it was didn't make a habit of moving that fast very often.

Huwhatttt! Hinto released his arrow.

"Dammit!" someone cursed a split second later.

"Reggie? Reggie?" It was the woman trying to kill me.

The man Hinto got with an arrow continued cursing, apparently not caring that he was drawing even more attention to himself.

"What's goin' on? Reggie?" the woman called out again.

"Damn Injun got me!"

The woman took a step forward and instantly disappeared, her scream following her. *Keh-pow!* Her pistol went off when she hit the bottom of the camouflaged hole.

I surely was glad me and Hinto had the foresight to set

the trap before we made camp for the night. I'd been bone-weary and didn't feel like going through the trouble, but it turned out to be time well spent.

I dropped the rock, happy I didn't have to throw it like some old caveman in the stories Ma used to tell me when I was a boy.

No more noise came from the hole. I'd feel bad if she broke her neck.

"Maude! Dammit!" the man named Reggie continued to curse and fumble around on the ground.

Lightning streaked across the sky in intermittent bursts. Another clap of thunder followed while I waited out Reggie's next move. I didn't have long to wait.

Cuh-lik ka-pow! The bullet took out a small chunk from the stone behind me. Apparently it took Hinto by surprise just like it did me.

"Throw down your gun," I said. "Keep shootin' and you're gonna kill Maude."

As he raced toward me, I got a bead on him.

Ka-pow-ow-ow! The shot echoed for what seemed forever. Through it all, I heard his gun land at his feet.

"Don't even think it, or you'll be chewin' the next bullet," I told him.

Hinto got to his feet and headed toward Reggie with another arrow at the ready.

"Maude!" Reggie started up again, wailing like a schoolboy.

"If he don't shut his yap, shoot him," I told Hinto as I lit a torch and took it with me. Hinto knew I wasn't serious, but Reggie didn't.

The crawl up the sloping boulders was more difficult than I anticipated because my hip was hurting like the blue blazes, and it was damp from the on again, off again mist. I picked my way through the few branches still covering the crevice and stopped at the edge of the trap.

Maude was sitting at the bottom, stunned-like and legs out in front of her, though she did look up when the light of my torch hit her. Then she frantically scrambled for her pistol at her feet.

"Toss it to me, real easy like. Unless you want my friend to finish Reggie off."

Her ensuing curse was way worse than Reggie's. It was the most unladylike word I'd ever heard; though I was careful not to let her think it bothered me. Travelers were hard people who knew how to needle you until they got what they wanted.

I had to remember that just because she was a woman, didn't mean she was a good person like Miss Cordelia or Patience. Liling had taught me that no matter how beautiful the package, the inside might be pure puss and rot.

My glance, though fixed on Maude, shifted to give the area around me a better look. It suddenly felt like Jaw-Long's daughter had me in her sights.

"Ya won't shoot him. Yer the jailer's son," she said with a sneer.

"Not anymore, I ain't," I said, moving the barrel of my Colt so it lined up with her forehead. I was truly tired of these games, woman or not.

"Maybe so," she said. "But Liling said ya didn't have it in ya to kill an innocent woman."

Chapter 2

Resurrection of Ghosts Past

I couldn't have been more stunned than if Maude turned into the hardnosed contortionist right in front of my eyes. Still, it wouldn't be to my benefit to show the woman her words had an effect on me.

I pulled back on the trigger of my revolver. "Guess she was wrong. On both counts."

Her eyes widened at the smooth click of the Colt's hammer. The torch was starting to burn a little lower than I liked, but it sure did a good job of illuminating the shocked look on her face.

Maude spat on the ground. "I say you won't," she almost dared me. "I'm a lady."

Now I remembered her. Hard lines framed her face, probably brought there by pure nastiness. She was one of the women who would never meet my eye when I looked at 'em. She never wasted an opportunity to spit on or near me when she had a chance.

I smiled. Let her think I was as scruple-less as her. It would only be to my advantage.

"Don't fit my definition of a lady by a long shot," I said evenly.

"Why you–" But she did put her hands up a little, as if she were about to surrender.

The fact she was being submissive didn't mean a hill of beans to me. She could have half-dozen weapons up her sleeve. Probably did.

"No wonder she wants ya dead," she grumbled.

My heart sped up for the merest of moments. Maude was most likely playing me, with her offhand comments about Liling, but I was one of those folks who didn't like loose ends. Real or imagined.

"You say it like she's alive."

"'Course she is!" she said. "Why else would I be here?"

When she grinned, the light from the torch accentuated the hard, dirty planes of her face, making her look feral.

My guts twisted a little. On occasion, even when I was awake, I'd thought about Liling's fate. Sometimes I pictured her riding off somewhere to heal. And while I was at it, I fantasized about her mind healin' too. But only because I wanted things to be good between her and Jaw-Long. It wasn't right that a father should have a child who had venom running through their veins.

I guess all my imagining was just that. Liling was alive and kickin' and apparently still rotten to the core if she still had people lookin' to kill me.

"Show him!" I heard Reggie call from just beyond our campfire. "Go on! Show 'im!"

I knew Hinto had him tied up. I also knew Reggie was scheming for a way to get him and Maude out of the pickle they were in.

"I ain't showin' this ass wipe nothin'," she groused, but not as loudly as she should have if she wanted Reggie to hear her.

Her words were meant for my ears alone. She wanted me to take the bait.

I had the benefit of position. I could wait forever for her to spill the beans on whatever it was the two of 'em were trying to titillate me with.

She narrowed her slitty eyes a tad more and suddenly made a move for her gun. I was ready.

Prack! The bullet that left my Colt hit the handle of her pistol, sending it skittering into the wall of her stone cell.

"Dammit!" she screeched, moving back like the gun was on fire. "That bullet coulda ricocheted!"

"What's goin' on over there?" Reggie called.

"I'd worry about yourself, if I was you," I said, not sparing him a glance.

I still didn't trust Maude. She didn't seem as scared as a normal woman would've, or should've, been. But then again, maybe the last year on her own, away from the show, had made her more stoic.

Suddenly she smiled. It wasn't pretty by a long shot. It said she had the upper hand, and it was a look I hated, whether it was real or pasted on.

"If I show it to ya, will ya turn us loose?"

"Why would I turn you loose? You'll just keep comin' back to cause harm to me and my friend."

She shook he head. It set her stringy hair to swinging. "Nope. I won't."

I didn't believe her for a second. It was getting dark. I still had to piss, and I didn't like standing out in the open. And now I had to figure out what to do with these two no-goods.

While I was getting fairly good at sleepin' with one eye open, I still didn't enjoy it. And now me and Hinto would have to share what little provisions we had with two people that wanted me to stop breathin'.

I quelled a sigh. "I thought you said Liling wanted me dead?"

She nodded. I waited for her to say more, but she just stared at me with her head cocked. She reminded me of one of my grandfather's vultures. And if there was one thing I didn't care for, useful or not, it was vultures.

"Just say what you gotta say."

The snide look on her face faltered, but quickly returned.

The nasty woman thought she had the upper hand! I didn't have a helluva lot of bullets left, but I'd happily go through a few more to get to the bottom of what I hoped would be the last of the travelers. By my account, there couldn't be too many show people left – if any at all – to pursue me after these two.

The moment my thumb moved to the hammer, her smug look disappeared.

"Throw the pistol up to my feet."

She wasn't happy, but obliged by moving cautiously to her feet, keeping her hands where I could see them. She gingerly picked up the pistol, letting it dangle by the trigger guard as she flung it up to me.

Cww-wuhhh. It landed near my boots with a softer sound because of the damp ground. I moved the weapon behind me with my heel.

"Maude? You all right?"

"Shut yer yap," I told Reggie without looking at him. Though Maude didn't have a weapon I could see, I had a feeling she wasn't done causing trouble.

I watched her turn to face me, keeping track of her sneaky hands.

"You say you don't want us dead, but you tried to kill us."

She twisted those thin lips of hers again. "If I wanted you dead, that's what you'd be."

I doubted it, but I guessed anyone could get lucky. My hip began to throb again, and I could hear Hinto and Reggie start to scuffle. I decided to end the preposterous situation once and for all.

"The next person that moves is gonna die," I said.

Miracle of miracles, both Maude and Reggie stilled.

"If ya promise to let us go, I'll show ya somethin' real special."

"All I gotta say is you're lucky I'm not someone else, 'cause I could just shoot you and take whatever it is you keep tellin' me about."

Her nostrils flared. As she moved back against the wall of her rocky prison, I got a waft of ammonia. She was either sick or hadn't washed her clothes or person for quite some time.

"Well?"

"Let me have a look at it then," I said, though I surely couldn't imagine what she had on her that was so special.

"Did ya show 'im yet?" Reggie called out.

Usually I'm not an impatient soul, but this never-ending blattin' about one thing or the other was startin' to wear on me.

"About to!" she called out. This time it was loud enough for her partner to hear.

I wondered if this back and forth business was some kind of trick, but with Reggie tied up, and Maude in a pit below me, I didn't see how either of 'em could get one over on me without bein' some kind of magician.

Maude dug around beneath her skirt and pulled out a little burlap bundle. I moved the torch. It didn't look like a thing that could hurt me.

"Toss it up."

"I been waiting a long time to give it to ya," she said with what could only be described as glee as she tossed it up.

It was too small to be a shrunken head, live snake, or anything else that could do my body harm. I tucked my Colt back in my holster, crouched down and untied the string that bound the burlap.

Beneath the glittering light of the torch, I unfolded first one side, then the other and unrolled it atop my knee.

My breath caught in my throat when the object was revealed.

It was the necklace I'd given Patience. Just to make sure, I turned it over and examined the charm and every link, as well as the clasp.

I tried really hard not to picture someone taking it off Patience, because I knew she would never willingly relinquish it. If I thought overly hard about what might have happened, it would only make me angry.

"How'd you come by this?" I asked as calmly as I could, though my blood felt like it had slowed in my veins.

Maude hooted. "Hee-hee! I knew it'd get yer goat!"

"Where did you get this?" I said each word separately and as calmly as I could. I tucked the necklace in my pocket and let the burlap fall to the ground.

There was a little part of me that didn't care that I said I'd let 'em go if they gave me what I wanted. Another part of me wanted to hurt her.

I brought my Colt out and pointed it down toward her when she didn't answer. Instead of shrinking back, she twisted her thin lips into a smile.

"Where do ya think?" For some reason, she seemed to think she had the upper hand now. "Liling said you'd be *real* happy to see it, but you kinda look troubled to me."

I doubted I had any expression on my face at all. Travelers liked to needle outsiders, so I just kept my insides as still as I could.

"Thought it was gonna be a sack o' gold," I said.

She looked taken aback for second. But only for a second.

"Got somethin' else, too," she said, her voice all giddy. "I bet this'll surprise ya."

"Well?" I said, when she didn't make a move to produce it. "Torch is almost out."

She didn't bother making any sort of face this time. She just reached down into her stocking again. The movement sent up another strong waft of ammonia. She had what looked like a ball inside her hand.

"Used to be clean," she muttered and tossed it right at me. It was lighter than I expected.

The moment I had it in my hand, I had a strange feeling come over me.

"Hoo-ee!" she crowed. "Ye're surprised *now*, ain'tcha, boy?"

It was a thin coil of hair, arranged in a braid. It was long and blonde and about a foot long. One end was straight as could be. It looked as if it had been removed with the precise slice of a sharp blade.

It made me wonder if the hair had been cut out this size on purpose. Or if the strand was only one piece of a whole lot of hair. But the most disturbing thing about the strand of dirty blonde hair was that I knew exactly where it had come from.

Patience.

Chapter 3

Worse

Maude stared up at me, her grimy brows knitted together, while all sorts of horrors played through my noggin.

It wasn't much of a stretch to picture Liling holding a knife to Patience's neck, or teasing the tip of her blade to my sweetheart's throat. I could even imagine Liling slicing a hunk of Patience's golden hair out of her head before she even knew what happened.

And that was the best situation I could come up with, so I forced myself to stop thinking about what had already transpired, and focus on the present.

"Ye said ye'd turn us loose!"

I glanced over at Reggie. This time Hinto had his hand on Reggie's shoulder. The traveler's hands were tied behind his back, and he was leaning slightly forward to compensate for his unnatural position. Hinto, as usual, had things under control.

"I don't know what I'm gonna do with the both of ya yet," I said. I truly didn't.

"Ya said–" Maude squawked.

"I don't care what I said. The more I think about it, the more I realize neither of you care a hill o' beans about anything but yerselves. You spent the better part of a year tracking me down just so you could put a bullet in my back. Far as I can tell, I never did either of you any harm."

That was the most that came out of my mouth in almost

a year, and it pretty much summed up my life during that time.

Ma used to say it didn't help thinking about what should've been. She said if you festered, you could never move forward to make things right just ahead of you.

There was a lot of truth in her words, though I was still seein' red about Patience and what she might have suffered because of my unwilling involvement with my evil grandfather and his traveling show.

"I promise we'll leave ya alone," she said.

When I looked down at her, she appeared as peaceable and sweet-faced as my own ma woulda looked.

I reluctantly placed the coil of golden hair in my pocket with the locket and tucked my Colt into my holster and lowered myself to one knee. I turned, so when I offered her a hand up, she couldn't take my revolver from me.

She grabbed my hand and steadied herself with her free one as I pulled her up and out. I felt the bones in her wrist and hand crack on the way up. The fact that her aging body was so filled with arthritis made me feel a twinge of sympathy for her even if she wasn't sweetest old lady I'd ever met.

Once she was on her feet, I looked down at her. She was shorter than I expected. She was also getting a hump on her back. Still, she was feisty despite all the troubles with her bones and such.

"It's about time," she said, moving past me, toward Reggie. Again, the stench of ammonia filled my nostrils, but I guess there were worse smells.

She turned back to me. "How'd ya like it if I threw *your* momma in there?" she snarled.

"She's dead," I said, not flinching. Outwardly, anyway.

"Hmmm." Her eyes softened a bit. She rubbed her shoulder, then skedaddled down the side of the damp boulder as agile as a mountain goat.

The torch was all but out. I quickly followed her so I

could make a new one.

Maude walked straight up to Hinto and Reggie like she was some kind of queen, instead of a smelly, bossy woman.

"Move back, Injun," she said. A split second later, a distant clap of thunder seemed to give her words more credence.

Hinto did as Maude ordered, probably to get out of the same space as her smelly person. Then, just as bold as you please, she untied her man.

"I'm hungry," was the first thing he said.

I still didn't trust Maude or her man, but I was in a more amenable mood now that I had some things of Patience's near me. I reached in my saddle bag and pulled out a couple sticks of dried venison.

"How about some Arbuckles to wash it down?" Maude asked, though it was more of an order than a question.

Once I set the pot on the fire, I turned back to face the silent pair. Hinto didn't look completely at ease, so I supposed I'd best get to the bottom of things before they turned nasty.

"So were ya gonna kill me without givin' me back my sweetheart's necklace, or not?" I asked.

Maude kept chawin' on the venison like it was a slab of juicy beefsteak. She shrugged after a moment.

"She said to kill ya when we was done." She sucked a string of meat out of her teeth. "Can't blame a crippled old woman for wantin' to save herself some time."

I surely didn't agree with her way of thinking, but I wasn't in her shoes so who was I to judge?

Reggie suddenly stopped chewin'. He looked a little sick. As if he was about to let go of what he just ate. He stared into the fire for a second and took a big swallow.

"She said she'd kill us both if we didn't find ya and give the necklace to ya."

I believed that much.

Maude turned to Reggie, her eyes narrowed. "I swear to Moses, you flap yer beak more than a whippoorwill."

He bowed his head and after a moment began chewin' slowly again.

"She finished our baby girl," he said in a whisper a moment later, his watery eyes moving up to meet my glance.

Maude put down what was left of her meat. Suddenly my stomach twisted, too.

"Isabel wasn't long for this world anyway," the old woman said, her gruff voice breaking.

"How do you know?" Reggie said, his eyes blazing as he turned to her. "My pa was in the coffin from scarlet fever and he started bangin' on the side of the box as we were lowerin' him into the dirt."

Maude swallowed hard and swiped at a tear that squeezed from the corner of her eye.

"She said it would be easier for Isabel." She took a few calming breaths. "But who would break a little girl's neck, for God's sake?" Her next words came out as a strangled whimper. "She's pure evil, that one."

Maude wasn't tellin' me anything I didn't know.

"Where's your horses?" I asked. They had to have come a long way on foot because neither me nor Hinto had heard any indication of horses other than Huàn and Hinto's paint pony.

"Horse. We only got one. He's about a mile back."

Steam was rising from the pot, so I took our two cups and filled 'em.

Maude and Reggie drank the scalding liquid like it was cool spring water. I guessed neither of 'em had much in the way of supplies. Not that me and Hinto had a surplus.

I saw Hinto take in the area around us from time to time, but it was also so surreptitiously that he could have been daydreaming for all anyone knew.

Reggie and Maude stared into the fire for a long moment, sighed in tandem like Ma and Pa used to do, then chewed up what was left of their meat and washed it down with the rest of their Arbuckle's.

"Don'tcha wanna know what she's got up her sleeve?" Maude asked.

"I figured you'd tell me if you thought it was something I should know," I said. "I'm not gonna beat it out of ya, if that's what you were thinkin'."

She gave me a long look from head to toe, then glanced over at Reggie, who lowered his face – like he was ashamed of himself for some reason.

"She sure has got a hate on you," she said, not bothering to look at me. "What'd ya do ta her?"

While me and Hinto were on the trail, I had a lot of time to ponder things. But my thoughts always seemed to come together into one thought: she was jealous of my relationship with Jaw-Long, and was worried that I might usurp her position in the show somehow. Not that it mattered anymore.

I shrugged.

"You got the better o' her," Reggie said, in a voice so low it was almost as if he was afraid Liling might hear it.

The way he hushed his voice would have been almost humorous, if his fear wasn't so palpable.

All the thoughts that were swirling' about in my noggin kinda settled into one: Liling knew that this day would come to pass eventually. She knew Reggie and Maude would find me. She knew we'd come face to face again, but I also knew they weren't through talkin'.

I added a couple sticks to the fire and all four of us sat around the fire for a while, watching sparks, listening to the crackle and hiss of the flames. Every now and again, the sound of a coyote would transcend the sounds of the fire, but for that it was peaceable.

"Much obliged if me and Reggie could sleep here to-night," Maude said.

The thought of sleepin' in such close proximity to the ammonia smell she gave off wasn't all that appealing, but there was something about her that was vulnerable. It made me want to look after her, like I would any woman.

I glanced at Hinto. He gave me an imperceptible nod.

"I won't slit yer throat," she said. "I swear it on my baby's grave."

"Won't slit yers, neither," I said. I went to my saddle bag and pulled out a smallish blanket and handed it to Maude.

She nodded, then put it about her shoulders, sending a smile my way as she did so.

I'm not gonna say she turned into a queen in the blink of an eye, but there was something almost ladylike about her features in the glow of the campfire.

"Thanks, Jailer's Son," she said in a soft voice. "Or whatever ye're callin' yerself these days."

I nodded and turned to make myself as comfortable as I could. Hinto offered his blanket to Reggie. The traveler looked a little fearful at first, but soon gave Hinto a grateful nod too.

As the fire died down and Reggie began snoring, Maude turned over and faced me.

"I was gonna wait 'til morning to tell ya, but we might not stay that long."

And with her words I knew I probably wasn't gonna like what she had to say. But before she even opened her mouth, a picture of Liling flashed through my mind. She was as pretty as I remembered, and smiling at me with one of those cruel half-smiles of hers.

That in itself gave me a start. But it was what my mind pictured next that really gave me pause. Lying on the ground at Liling's feet was a body covered in silk. Alive? Dead? I didn't have a clue. I only knew it wasn't moving.

But the biggest shock: beyond Liling, was a girl in a dress with blonde hair piled atop her beautiful head. Her hands were bound in front of her and a rag covered her mouth. Her blue eyes were weeping tears, and I just knew the tears were meant for me.

The girl? It was Patience, though she looked like a growed woman.

"I don't know what day it is, but Liling said ya were gonna have a bad homecoming if you missed the Deadwood Fourth of July celebration," Maude said.

Her words jarred me out of my dark thoughts, into an even darker one: Me and Hinto didn't see many towns – mainly because we went out of our way to avoid trouble. I was pretty sure, however, that it was near the end of June.

There was no way in hell I was gonna make it to Deadwood before the Fourth of July shindig.

Chapter 4

Hell Bent For Leather

More than a year had gone by since I'd seen Liling. What if the Fourth of July celebration she was referring to was last year?

"How long ago did you talk to her?" I asked Maude.

"Well ... she found us a few months after we left the show." She seemed to be trying to mentally calculate how long it was. After a few seconds she shrugged. "A half a year or more. I kinda lost track of time."

That meant she was referring to the upcoming Fourth of July, 1889. There was still a chance I could make it to Deadwood in time. I hated to ask so much of Huàn, but I knew he was at his best when he was doing his best for me.

I stood and turned toward Hinto, who had silently been taking in the exchange.

"You go now," Hinto said with a slow nod of his head. His dark, smooth face showed no emotion.

I nodded. "You comin' with me?"

He shook his head.

I held out my hand. "I want to thank you, my friend."

Hinto got to his feet. He clasped me to his chest as a father would a son.

Then I turned to saddle Huàn. If I thought he would be wanting to rest, I was in for a surprise. He was rarin' to go. I'm guessing he knew I wouldn't saddle him back up again after a day of riding if there wasn't a good reason for it.

"Ye're not gonna leave us here alone with that Injun, are ya?" Maude asked. She had the wherewithal to look nervous. And she shoulda been after her little jabs about him.

"I sure am. But only because you showed me some kindness in the end."

My words threw her for a loop, but if she had even a speck of sense, she'd know I was doin' her a favor.

Huàn nickered when I brought my saddle over his back. He seemed genuinely happy that we were goin' on an adventure alone, and when there were stars in the sky to boot.

We had the best part of the moon to guide us, and the higher it rose, the more help it would be. I sure didn't want to have Huàn step in a ground squirrel hole or disturb a rattler out for a midnight nibble.

Hinto joined me while I cinched the saddle.

"Your pa good man," Hinto said.

I wasn't sure what brought out his kind words on behalf of my pa, but it was a nice gesture on his part. I knew Pa had probably done some questionable things in his past, but I guessed not a one of us could say we hadn't either.

"He give me back Tasunke. My son," he said in that halting way of his. I liked the cadence of his words. It gave me time to really digest the importance of what he had to say.

When I finished tugging on the saddle to make sure it was snug, I turned toward Hinto. His face was as impassive as ever, but there was a sadness to it, too.

"How'd that come to pass?" I asked. I knew he meant Pa had brought Tasunke's dead body back to him.

"Soldiers shoot in back."

It was only a guess, but I imagine Pa somehow tried to stop the event, or tried to help Tasunke once he'd been wounded, but failed. Pa had brought the brave's body back as a courtesy to Hinto. I still didn't know how Hinto and Pa knew each other in the first place, and I doubted I ever would. I guessed it really didn't matter.

The short exchange between me and Hinto brought home the fact that Hinto still must've felt his debt to my pa wasn't paid in full. Or maybe Hinto simply thought of me as his own son now that I didn't have no pa. Either way, I was happy he decided to forsake his people to look after my hide when I needed it.

"Sorry about your son."

Words could not express my gratitude for all Hinto had done and been for me, but it was time to release him from what he thought was his duty.

"You've been my teacher," I said, placing a hand on his shoulder. "My friend. My father." I paused to swallow the sudden lump in my throat.

"I will never be able to repay you, but it's time to be with your people, Hinto." I looked down into his eyes for a long moment. I remembered a time when we'd been eye to eye. I must've growed a good three or four inches the past year.

"It would be an honor to see you again, though. And it goes without sayin' that if you ever need a thing, I will walk barefoot through hell and back to see that you get it."

He reached under his buckskin top and withdrew the necklace that matched the one he'd given me. He brought it to his forehead and then back to his heart.

I briefly placed my hand over my heart, then hopped on-to my saddle and headed away from camp in a southeasterly direction, my heart heavy with sadness and dread.

Sadness because I knew that Hinto bringing the necklace to his head and then his heart meant he figured there was a chance we'd never see each other again.

Dread because the vision of Patience seemed to be moving farther from me.

It was pretty much nothingness around me and Huàn the first day. I barely saw a critter, let alone a human person.

Huàn sensed my urgency and gave me what he had. We

28

stopped for water and short rests as much as we were able, but nothing more. From the moment I rode away from camp, my sense of urgency began to build.

I kept picturing that sheet of silk covering a body near Liling, and the more I thought about it, the more I just knew the body under it was a dead one. The image of Patience's face too, became grimmer the longer I rode. I just couldn't get her sparkling, tear-filled eyes out of my head.

And then, as I was deep in thought, the rooftops of a town came into view. The sun's early morning rays slanted off the dew-covered wood shingles making them look like pieces of a dirty mirror.

Weighing the wisdom of stopping in town, versus going around, I decided to stop in just for a minute. First off, I needed to see what day it was. I also needed to purchase a few things at the general store and get a treat for Huàn.

I still had some coins from George's hidden cache that I kept on me in case of an emergency such as this. Raoul split what he called our "birthright" with me when we parted ways, and I immediately gave my half of that to Hinto. I tried to give the entire thing to Hinto because it was blood money as far as I was concerned, but he accepted half, and that was the end of that.

Before I left the show for the last time, I watched Raoul, still in bad shape himself, handing out pouches to the other members of the show. It was good to know that George's wickedness hadn't won out in the end.

The smell of home-cooked vittles made my stomach growl as I neared the small group of buildings, but it also instantly made me homesick for Miss Cordelia and Jaw-Long's cooking. I couldn't help but smile when I thought about Patience's grandma teaching her to cook too. Soon I hoped to sample all their cooking.

Huàn huffed a bit at the perimeter of town, and began sidestepping as he made his way to the center of town. If he'd been any other horse, I would've dug my heels into his sides to stop him from balking, but Huàn was no ordinary horse. He sensed things above and beyond what I did, and it seemed I was always on the alert for some sort of trouble. Maybe that was why we ended up together like we did.

"What's wrong?" I asked Huàn, my eyes and ears trying to pick up something out of the ordinary. And then my stomach did a little flip-flop.

Three men on horseback appeared and rode into the middle of the rutted road, creating a barrier to me entering the sleepy town.

It had been my experience that towns such as these were usually wary of lone riders, and riders who entered on a full gallop, but today it was almost as if I was expected, and that was a peculiar thought, indeed.

Huàn tossed his head and snorted a couple times.

"I know, Huàn. I know," I told him softly.

He didn't like the situation any more than I did. I reined up; more to give me time to think about what my options were than anything else.

I guessed I didn't really need to go into town. I could make do until the next one, but now I was interested in the reason why men on horseback would come meet a stranger at this early time of day.

It wasn't that I was so full of myself that I thought they were there because of me. It was just the pure strangeness of seeing the almost sentinel-like pose of three men on horseback, backs so stiff they looked like they had a stick holding 'em up.

About a hundred yards away from the men on horseback, me and Huàn stopped where we were. He switched his tail while I moved my head ever so slightly to take in as much of the area around me as I could. Even if I didn't have one iota of intuition in me, I knew something wasn't right.

The men looked like ordinary ranch hands. Maybe they

were newly-minted deputies, though that still didn't explain what they were doin' at the gates. Then I saw something so strange that my mind took note of it. There was a boy in the small cemetery at the entrance of town, running right down the middle of it. Suddenly, like someone put up an invisible wall in front of him, he stopped. Then he turned and stared at me for a second before sticking out his tongue at me.

The boy's rude gesture didn't throw me for a loop – I'd seen way stranger things than that, but it did make me wonder if he'd been the one to warn the men on horseback that I was comin'.

A more logical explanation was that they liked to sort through visitors to make sure none brought any trouble into town with them. I'd seen that very thing a time or two, but had never had to pass by a group of three men before, in one tight clump. They all had rifles in their hands, at the ready, but none of them had their weapon pointed at me, so that was a good thing.

Despite that, I couldn't completely put the uneasy feeling I had about the situation aside. Yet, the longer I dawdled, the weaker I appeared. And worse, the longer I dawdled, the longer it would take to reach Deadwood and to reach Patience.

I nudged Huàn's side. He huffed a bit, but did what I told him. As he started trotting closer to the trio, a pain shot through my forearm.

It was where Chester got me. An entire year had gone by, but it still caused me grief from time to time. Though I'd practiced shooting 'til I was blue in the face, my aim never did return to what it had been. The sudden pain seemed to be a warning to remember my limitations.

The man in the middle suddenly held up his hand, and I reined up. I was close enough now to see that he was a young man with a long blonde mustache. He had the bearing of someone who was, or had been, in the military.

"Just passing through," I said. "Don't want no trouble."

The man said nothing, just stared at me. They all did. The boy in the cemetery, though he was far away, did the same. Huàn took a couple steps to the side. He was gettin' antsy, and I was startin' to feel the same way.

I don't like feeling off balance. That's when I noticed I started makin' mistakes.

Nothing was getting accomplished as far as I could tell, and even if the three men were fair to middlin' marksmen, I was outnumbered. I didn't know what was in that small stain of a town that they were so keen to protect, but whatever it was, I didn't want to know.

Just as I was about to give Huàn a nudge to head away from the Mexican standoff, an open carriage appeared behind the three men on horses.

There was an almost orchestrated feel to the whole scene playing out in front of me. I might have been exiled from the world for a year, but a man never forgot the nuances and oddities of a situation that were usually harbingers of trouble. And right now, I knew I was in trouble.

One of the horsemen moved aside, and the carriage drove between the horses, straight toward me. As it did so, the other two men moved their rifles from at the ready to right straight at me.

Maybe I'd been gone from civilization too long because my mind truly struggled to comprehend what was happening.

I did know that whoever was in the carriage was of some importance. Otherwise, the men wouldn't have been so deferential. Perhaps they worked for the man in the carriage. The man and the woman, I amended when I saw a fan hiding a face next to the man.

As the carriage drew near, and the men on horses followed it, dread filled me. I would've added fear, too, but I couldn't be sure until I saw what I hoped wasn't possible. The open carriage stopped a short distance in front of me. Huàn whinnied then. It was a warning whinny, but it came too late.

My gaze moved to the passengers inside the carriage. The man was what appeared to be a dandy. He turned toward the woman, and she lowered her fan. The smell of intoxicating flowers suddenly hitting me like a brickbat.

Though I was careful not reveal it, my dread and fear finally had a name:

Liling.

More Surprises

"That's Maxwell Beck," Liling said. While she spoke, the man beside her regarded me much as he might a cur dog.

"He's not much more than a skinny boy," he said with a snigger.

"Looks can be deceiving."

"I don't know who ya think ya are, but I don't know anyone of ya," I said with a shrug.

The dandy look surprised for a second. He snapped his gaze toward Liling, but she never took her eyes off me.

"It is Maxwell Beck. Check his pockets. You will find a clover charm necklace. It was mine. He stole it from my father."

Damn! I thought. *She didn't change one bit.* But she had. She looked different somehow, a little fuller in the face because her fine cheekbones weren't so pronounced.

"I told you he would be along presently," she said in perfect English.

I purely didn't know how Liling could know such a thing when I didn't know it myself, but here I was.

"Take him to the jail," the dandy said.

My heart skipped a beat. Huàn felt my distress and took a step backward. It was his way of saying he would give it his all. I only needed to give him the signal.

Unfortunately, we were too close to Liling and the men on horses. Even if only three of 'em had guns, one had a fairly good chance of putting a bullet in me or in Huàn, and I wasn't gonna risk my faithful friend's life in such a foolhardy manner.

Then, as my brain was taking in every bit of my surroundings, weighing my options, my hearing abruptly left me.

Astounded, I tried to cover my shock and distress as best as I could. I say shock because my body and senses had been slowly healing since me and Hinto rode away from what was left of the show.

After the dynamite incident, which left both George and Chester dead, my hearing seemed to mend on its own. I chalked it up to bein' free to heal in a mostly safe environment. Hinto said one of his people had the same thing happen to him during battle. The brave's hearing sometimes left him in times of great stress, only to return when he didn't especially need it.

I sure hoped I wasn't gonna be like that brave Hinto told me about. If so, things were gonna get unpleasant for both me and Huàn in a hurry.

My eyes focused on the dandy. While I knew Liling was the real chief of the group, the man beside her was the one giving voice to her orders.

Hands up! the dandy suddenly barked, the string tie laying against his chest bobbing as he strained forward in his seat. At least that's what his lips said. I still couldn't hear him. His face instantly turned red, except for a couple of white spots that bracketed his mouth.

His voice must've been loud because the two horses pulling the carriage lurched forward. Liling caught the reins and wrenched them back before the man beside her could react.

I slowly raised my hands and exhaled slowly before taking a steadying breath. Huàn tensed; he knew this wasn't a good situation. If we were separated, he was gonna have to go somewhere he didn't wanna go. I just hoped no one mistreated him – for their sake.

"Why?" I asked in a careful but undaunted voice. If I were overly loud, Liling would know that I couldn't hear. I surely didn't want her to know about any weakness, no matter how small.

Murder, the dandy answered for her.

It was pretty much what I expected. Will had come to the traveling show at his own peril to tell me that much.

"Who?"

My father, Liling said.

I had plenty of time to think about the two words that came out of Liling's mouth when I was in the hoosegow. First off, the vision I had of a man at Liling's feet, covered with silk, did indicate that she finally got the better of him. But I didn't have that awful feeling I usually got when something was as bad as it could get. But was it only because I had made Jaw-Long invincible in my thoughts?

Everyone said I was fast with a gun, but Jaw-Long was just as fast, and better with blades of any kind. It was darned near impossible to think that someone got the better of him.

Of course, all my thoughts circled back to Patience. She was the reason I was headed back to Deadwood in the first place. She was the reason my heart ached at the thought of being cooped up and unable to get to her.

Still, I reasoned, if Liling was here, she wasn't in Deadwood, able to do harm to Patience. And me and Hinto had dispatched pretty much all of the traveling show members that had come after us, so I felt fairly certain Patience was as safe as she could be at present.

Just like that, my hearing came back, as crisp and clear as you please. So clear, it seemed to me I could hear more than before, if such a thing was even possible, but maybe it was only because I was both thankful and relieved.

I even heard two men out in the front of the jail, jawin'

about the jailer's son. Bad news really did travel fast. The tail end of their conversation: "...ain't gonna last long." I heard a cackle out of one 'em, then the sound of the front door opening, and a murmured warning from the deputy. The soft scuffle of boots along the plank boardwalk followed.

Swinging my legs up onto the cot so I was as comfortable I could be on the lumpy, dirty pad, I tried to think myself out of my predicament. I took in the bare beams above me with spaces between the roof boards where the tarpaper didn't cover it. The sharp ends of nails poked through here and there, too. Whoever erected the building had clapped it together in a hurry.

It wasn't difficult to picture this room getting chilly in the winter and hot in the middle of summer. The sheriff's office would be easy to burn or tear down, too. That was one reason so many buildings in Deadwood were now built from stone quarried right outside the city proper, and also out of sandstone from Hot Springs.

The glass that usually would've covered the space outside the bars was gone. It might have been removed at Liling's request, but it was probably because the weather was tolerable. The steel bars were unbendable and too close together to wiggle through.

Which meant I had to find a way to get my hands on a key or a gun, or have someone pay the law to turn the other way. But I knew the latter wasn't a possibility. Liling wasn't gonna let me slip out of her hands now that she had them around my neck. I got myself into this mess. I'd get myself out.

A few moments later, the door to the jail proper opened.

"Stay back," said one of the men who had greeted me at the town's entrance. He shoved a biscuit and what looked like some greasy meat through a slot near the floor. Then he slid a tin mug of water behind it.

The whole time he kept his holstered gun side away from

me. Apparently everyone had been warned about me.

I grinned to myself. Stories had a way of exponentially growing. If I were handy with a gun in real life, the story goin' around probably had me unarming a dozen men at once with one of my hands tied behind my back.

My stomach was growlin', so I got up and ate the biscuit and side pork. It was more than palatable, and the biscuit was made fresh this morning. Put together, it was a welcome change from my typical diet of beans and meat of one sort or another.

I took my time drinking my water as I listened to the town beginning a new day.

Whooooophsh. Whooooophsh. The was the sound of bellows exhaling in the livery.

Clwang! Clang-clang! The blacksmith pounded a thinnish horseshoe. In between those sounds, I heard a horse noisily slurping water out of a trough somewhere nearby. Don't know why, but I really liked that sound. And then I heard the best one of all: Huàn.

He was giving someone a hard time, and it did my heart good. He was the opposite of me in a woolly situation. While I would sort through things, then try to piece them together to figure out the whole, Huàn was impatient. He tried to force things into some semblance of order.

I heard the main door to the sheriff's office open. There was a long pause and then I heard a pair of boot heels on the floor.

The pause meant someone with soft soles had entered. The fact that hard heels followed most likely indicated that a woman had entered first.

Since the only woman I'd seen so far in this town was Liling, I figured it was probably her and the dandy the deputies referred to as *sheriff.* I still didn't see how a dandy like that could be sheriff, but there were crooked folks in all walks of life.

The flames flickered inside the kerosene lamps against the wall that formed the partition between this room and the office. Whoever was outside decided it was time to visit me.

An instant later, the door to the jail opened, fanning the pungent smell of kerosene over to me. It nearly overpowered the smell of flowers that I associated with Liling, but not completely.

I leisurely swung my legs over the cot to face my callers, though leisurely was the last thing I felt.

"I trust you are as comfortable as you can be despite your circumstances?" Liling said, walking inside, with the sheriff at her side.

While she sized me up, I took the opportunity to do the same. Liling was still a beauty. She seemed a little thicker, but that might have been because of the poufy high society dress with all the trimmings she was wearing. I noticed a couple other changes, too.

She had another scar on her face, behind the scar on her cheek. It had the look of a shrapnel wound. It was well-concealed, but I knew it had caused her great pain.

As she shifted forward, I noticed her right arm wasn't moving in synchronicity with the rest of her. It seemed a bit stiff. In her present condition, I doubted she was still able to execute those fancy contortionist moves she used to be so dern good at.

"I suppose so," I said.

"You know why you're being held here, don't you, boy?" the sheriff asked. I saw two points of a badge peeking out from beneath his overcoat.

"She said I killed her father."

"If she said you killed her father, then you killed her father," he said, irritation creeping into his voice.

"That'll be up to the jury to decide," I said.

When his lip curled, I decided to push the issue. "You're a lawman. It's your duty to uphold the law."

"As a lawman, it's my duty to dispense with justice as I see fit."

And with those words, I knew there was nothing else I could say one way or the other. Liling had worked her magic on him. He should've said, "As a lawman, it's my duty to follow the law and see justice done."

My fate was sealed. Liling was gonna finally get her revenge. In a roundabout way, it would hurt me twice as much because she knew I respected the laws of men.

"Can I take a look at the warrant?"

The sheriff screwed up his shiny mug. "Just who in the hell do you think you are, ordering me around like some servant?"

I'd asked, not ordered, but there wasn't a word I could say that wouldn't egg him on or irritate him. Still, I had to try to get his thoughts back on his duties.

"A man who wants to see proof of his charges," I said. "I saw telegraph wire to the north, so I'm thinkin' recent proof shouldn't be too difficult to come by." I paused. *"If* you're even one tiny bit serious about upholding your duties as a lawman."

"You are an uppity one," the sheriff said.

"I'm no better 'n anyone else. But like anyone else, I have a right to due process." I paused to let my words sink in. "If I can't have Chase Beck, the sheriff over in Deadwood for my legal counsel, I'd like to retain an attorney from this, or any neighboring town."

"With what?" Liling finally said, her words sharp with irritation.

"The gold coin I rode in with should be sufficient for a start."

"What gold coin?" the sheriff asked, eyes narrowed. It might have meant he was irritated that he hadn't been informed about any gold, but it mostly meant he was interested because he was a greedy man.

Liling gave me a long look, flicked a glance up at the sheriff who still hadn't divulged his name, then turned and soundlessly left the room.

Again, I noticed a slight stiffness to her arm and a bulkiness about her chest.

As the sheriff moved close to the bars that separated us, I pictured myself simultaneously thrusting my hands through them and grabbing the sides of his face. Preferably his ears because they were tender. Once I had his head in my hands, I'd bring it against the metal rods with enough force to knock him out cold. As he slid, unconscious to the floor, I'd remove him of his gun and keys, and then use them to make my escape.

Of course it was only a fantasy. He had one of his knucklehead deputies just past the doorway, keeping an eye on him.

"I'd get the idea of a trial out of your head, jailer's son," he said. "You've already been declared guilty of three counts of capital murder. The sheriff seemed to savor the word, murder. Then he smiled. Behind him, the door to the office opened and closed almost noiselessly.

"Day after tomorrow, you'll be swinging at the end of a rope."

Chapter 6

Hanging

If I was surprised, it was only because he took so long to say what I figured was coming. Of course they wanted to hang me. Otherwise, it would give anyone that gave two hoots about me time to arrange a legal hearing. Outsiders getting involved would destroy Liling's dreams of seeing me hang from a noose, legs twitching and eyes bugged out of my skull.

"Then I respectfully request a signed writ of my guilt, and would also ask that the judge who signed the writ be made aware of the fact that I am now available in person to protest my guilt."

The sheriff's eyes widened and his head shifted back on his neck. He wasn't used to havin' someone tell him how to do his job.

"And again, I should like to know your name," I continued. "We've never been formally introduced. The only proof I have that you are indeed a lawman is just a glimpse of your badge."

The sheriff's face twisted. "My wife warned me you were a forthy one."

Liling was his wife! The man was more of a dolt than I figured. He didn't know how lucky he was to be alive right now, but I guess she had a use for him. Once her work was done, I had no doubt she'd discard him like she did everyone else – or worse.

This was where both sides of me warred over what to do. Arguing would only make it difficult to accomplish anything. But if I kept my mouth shut, he would believe I was all the things Liling told him I was.

"Well?"

He stared at me for a long minute, then moved his coat aside so I could see the full glory of his shiny badge. Looked like he spent all mornin' spit-shinin' it.

"Sheriff Buford Benedict." He turned to his deputy, grinned, and then faced me. "At your service," he said, sarcasm drippin' off his words.

Then, with a chuckle, he left.

I sat back down on the cot and immediately looked up at the ceiling, examined the floorboards, and checked the walls for their constitution and age. Then I gauged distances from every point in the room as best I could. Once I finished cataloging every thought and figure of the lodgings, I laid my head down on the lumpy mattress to take a snooze.

I had two days to get myself outta my mess, and I was gonna need my strength.

I must've been wore right out because I fell fast asleep and had a vivid dream, unlike any I'd had before. This dream held me prisoner in its wretched embrace, torturing me with all my shortcomings.

The faces of those I loved filed past me while I took in their expressions of sadness, anger, and impotence. Ma, looking like an angel without wings, offered me a sad, sweet smile.

What's wrong, Ma? I had to think the words, because my mouth wouldn't work. When I reached up to touch my mouth, I realized it was sewn shut with yarn. Oddly, the yarn stitches didn't hurt, but they surely put a damper on communicatin'.

Ma just looked back at me with those big, sad eyes of hers

and shook her head. Then she was gone.

Pa came next. If I had to say what sort of mood he was in, I'd peg it as frustrated. He looked like he wanted to do something, but couldn't. Then his eyes implored me to take action. *What, Pa?* I wanted to ask, but of course my mouth was sewed shut.

A lariat suddenly snaked into my line of vision and fell over the top of my head. I realized it wasn't no lariat at all. It was a hanging noose, and it was meant for me.

Then I saw my Uncle Turtle, Miss Cordelia, Sarge, Phin, and James. Their faces held a mixture of emotions. Sarge looked as anxious as I'd ever seen him. And I just knew the anger on Uncle Turtle and Miss Cordelia's faces wasn't directed toward me, it was *about* me. I also knew their anger had to do with that dern hanging rope.

Jaw-Long was next. He just stared me. What did that mean? Not long ago, I pictured him on the ground, still as death and covered with silk. Now he was on his feet, and lookin' like he was made out of a big block o' lake ice.

I wasn't a seer by any stretch of the imagination, but I knew my dreams about Jaw-Long either meant he was dead or powerless. They were that strong.

Finally, I saw Patience. She wore a long face with tears trickling down her pretty pink cheeks. This time, like the last time I pictured her, she appeared all grown up. She wore her hair in ringlets atop her head. I had such a clear picture of her, I even saw a beautiful hair comb keeping those curls of hers in place.

But that wasn't all I saw.

As she seemed to glide away from me, I got a better picture of what was goin' on. I saw Liling in the background. She, too, looked different. She moved toward Patience with an angry expression and grabbed her by the hair and pulled her along toward the back of the room.

It was then I realized this was a saloon. But it wasn't just an ordinary saloon. It was a house of ill repute. How did I know? Because above the sound of lively piano and somewhat discordant banjo strumming, I heard the sounds of a drunk calling out her name, "Patience, honey!"

My body struggled against the invisible bonds that held me, and I fought to close the distance between me and her. I had to reach her before the man did. I was gonna keep her from his disgusting grasp if it was the last thing I did.

Her fingertips reached out to me. I watched my hand strain to capture her fingers in mine. Just as we were about to come together, I heard a jarring voice:

"Practicing' for what's comin', day after tomorrow?"

The voice belonged to Sheriff Benedict. And as I blinked the dream away, I saw he had a smile on his face, but it was pleasant, as if he was asking if I was getting ready to join an ice cream social instead of preparing to meet my Maker. When I didn't answer, he said:

"Unfortunately for you, I don't think our Lord and Savior has much mercy for unrepentant criminals."

I tried to pull myself together, but I felt damp from sweat and unsettled to the bottoms of my feet. Once I swung my legs nonchalantly over the side of the cot, I faced him.

"You here for a reason?"

The sheriff arched an eyebrow at me. "You are one cool cucumber. It would appear that at least some part of your reputation is deserved."

I said nothing. The door swooshed closed with a soft thud as he seated himself in a high back chair. He stared at me for a long moment. "You have a last request?"

I might not be a man of many words, but I guessed the ones I said next would be pretty important to my future.

"Well," I said. "Remember the gold I was tellin' you about?"

At the mention of the word, *gold*, I could tell I piqued his interest. Few men could resist the thought of getting their hands on some. Heck, it was all Will talked about when he wasn't talking about some pretty girl.

"I don't have all day," he said, sounding irritated as some tired schoolmarm.

"I hid a sack of it, about twenty miles west o' here."

Sheriff Benedict blinked a couple of times. Then he shifted and swallowed hard. I could practically see his brain doin' calculations. He wanted the gold for himself, but he couldn't tell Liling about it. Just the fact that he paired off with that wicked woman meant he was as black-hearted as she was. Even so, his mind was plottin' how he could get his hands on it without anyone else knowin' about it. He was just like every other man with no scruples.

"Looks like you're gonna die without it," he said finally.

Those were the words I expected to fall out of his mouth. I also knew he was gonna try his darndest to wrest that imaginary gold from me before I hung, one way or another.

"Suppose I probably will," I said, scratching behind my ear. I hadn't washed in two days, and I was starting to feel gritty from the ride and then sweatin' after that awful dream.

"Then why did you mention it?" he asked.

I shrugged. I was beginning to enjoy this game. The way I saw it, toying with this miserable excuse of a human being was pretty much all I had left. I was in a town I didn't even know the name of. I didn't have my guns. Some stranger was holding onto Huàn, probably already imagin' him as his own horse. Patience was likely in dire straits, and all my loved ones were far, far away.

He exhaled suddenly, then stood and pivoted on the heels of his shiny new boots. "I don't have time for nonsense," he said as he started walking.

"I'll split it with you, if you send my uncle my final words. I'm gonna have to see proof of an answer from him, though."

The sheriff paused for a long moment. Then he left me.

46

After stretching, I went to the window, feeling a little better about the situation. Benedict, for all his smug disdain, was interested in my offer. Very interested.

I went to the window and sucked in some fresh air. At the aroma of baking fowl, my stomach growled. I also smelled sour dough, and Arbuckle's.

After another nonchalant stretch, I placed my hands on the bars atop the window opening. To the untrained eye, it would look like I was leaning wearily against the metal bars, contemplating my fate. In reality, I was gauging the possibility of an escape through the fortified portal.

It had been surprisingly easy to escape from the jail in Deadwood before I'd given it a look to see where security could be improved. This small-town jail was nowhere near as big or well-built.

There wasn't really any give to the bars, but I wasn't surprised. Jailbirds tended to focus all their energy on trying to escape through the front of their cell via the door, or through the rear, via a window. That's why those two places were usually the most fortified places in a jailhouse. The roof would probably be my best bet.

It didn't pay for me to look up again. It would only raise suspicion if someone were keepin' a sly eye on me. While I'd been in exile, I'd spent most of my time healing, instead of training. I hadn't run up a wall or building in a coon's age.

The wall of the cell was made of bars, too, and they were strong. If need be, I could shimmy up to the ceiling, using the strength of the bars as a help instead of a hindrance. But once I got to the ceiling, I wasn't sure how I was gonna get through the roof, poor construction or not.

While I was plotting, I heard a woman's voice, yodeling just as loud as you please. As she neared the jail, I realized it was Maude. It sounded like she was trying to attract attention to herself for whatever reason.

It wasn't the smartest move. Someone like her wasn't

gonna be welcome in a town like this, even without singing like they were trying to be a whole church choir all by their lonesome. And then there was the matter of Liling.

"Where are ya, boy?"

Now that surprised me. She was looking for me.

While my brain tried to figure out if I should stay quiet or call out to her, the door to the jail opened. My dilemma ended just that quick.

"I've got a proposition for you," Sheriff Benedict said, again closing the door tight behind him.

"What's that?" I asked, trying to sort out the sounds behind me.

"You can tell me where the gold is, and I'll see to it that your body is delivered to Deadwood via train."

"I may be young, but I wasn't born yesterday," I told him. "Once I'm dead, there's no one here to make sure you carry out your end of the deal."

I heard Maude's voice rise up an octave outside the jail as she yelped, "Hello? Hell-oh-oh! Hey? Anybody hear me?"

Sheriff Benedict narrowed his eyes in irritation. Then I heard her say, "Someone better take me to my boy this instant!"

Could she be talking about me? I wondered. She had to be!

The sheriff took his attention from Mabel and focused it all on me. "I have no assurances, either. If you were anyone else, I would have dismissed your words as a fabrication the moment they came out of your mouth." He paused. "But you have a reputation for telling the truth, so I thought I'd give you a chance to redeem yourself."

Redeem *my*self? The statement was almost laughable.

"You have absolutely nothing to lose," I reminded him. "You'll be a rich man if you carry out your end of the deal. You won't have to lean on your wife."

His nostrils flared at the affront to his manhood. "My

wife is under my care."

"Whatever you say," I told him with a shrug.

Maude's voice was now a shrill scream.

"Shut that bitch up!" Sheriff Benedict hollered toward the front of the jail. Looked like Maude was getting under his collar. That and maybe the thought of havin' a sack o' gold slip out of his hands before he even touched it.

The sound of hurrying footsteps and the slam of the outside office door followed.

"So what's it gonna be?" he asked after he regained his composure, but his mood had soured.

"You know," I told him. "I don't think I need your help no more." I felt my mouth twitch into a slight smile despite my dire circumstances.

"What's that supposed to mean?"

"I hear my dear ol' ma outside. I'm finished talkin' about my gold."

Chapter 7

Playing With Fire

Sheriff Benedict's jaw dropped. Mine would've, too, if I'd been in his shoes.

"Your ma is dead," he said when he recovered.

"What kind of fool would say such a blasphemous thing? Everyone knows I killed my pa, but I didn't do nothin' to my sweet ol' ma," I said.

If the sheriff wasn't taken aback by my words, I'm sure the angry look on my face threw him for a loop.

"Li–" He stopped and cleared his throat.

I'm sure the pause was designed to give him time to think up his next words. "The story is, *both* your parents are dead."

"That's the trouble with stories. Lots of 'em are just that." I gave my head a little shake, like I was disgusted. "I always wondered how stories like that get started. It ain't like Ma bein' dead would help anyone."

Now the sheriff really looked confused. I was sure he was picturing his plans unraveling, and was trying to figure out a way to salvage them.

I turned away, and when I did, I heard Huàn's throaty whinny. It was distant, so I knew he had to be a good block away. Still, it did my heart good to hear that my friend was still as lively. While I didn't figure there was a way he could help get me outta jail, he certainly could get me *away* once I got myself free.

Ma used to say necessity was the mother of invention.

My lie about the gold didn't go as planned, probably because I wasn't a liar by nature. Still, I needed to save my bacon, so I was just gonna hope that Maude might have some trick up her sleeve. If not, I'd have to whip up another falsehood.

And, on the off-chance that I was readin' Maude's comin' here the wrong way, I would call her a liar and let the sheriff try to untangle the web of lies – hers and mine.

"Why would I listen to a pup like you over a woman like Liling?"

I smiled then and gave my head a little shake.

"What's that supposed to mean?" he growled.

"Not much, I suppose. You're still kickin', ain't ya? If ya been with yer wife for any length of time and ye're still breathing..." I trailed off on purpose so he could mull my words.

"Sonny!" It was Maude again, and her timing couldn't have been more perfect.

Sheriff Buford Benedict was with me the entire time the old woman had been calling for me, and he hadn't heard me prompt her. I was certain I'd planted a real seed of doubt in his mind, and it made my heart glad.

I turned toward the window and went to it.

"In here, Ma!" I called. "They got me in the hoosegow!"

"Stop your hollerin', woman!" the sheriff called toward the window. I watched a dull shade of red creep up from Benedict's collar to color his freshly-shaved cheeks.

I shrugged and turned back to face him.

"Be right there, honey!" Maude called in a voice so cheery that I had to force myself to keep the surprise off my puss.

"I don't know what kind of game you're playing, Jailer's Son, but I'd be careful if I were you. Just because I said I was gonna hang you tomorrow, don't mean I won't do it today."

"You're running the show, not me," I told him. As he turned to leave, I said, "Liling spend all that gold she inherited from my grandpa? Sure was a lot of it."

He turned back and I saw the red from his cheeks had now crept up around his eyes. It looked like someone hung him upside down for a while, and only just now set him on his feet.

"It truthfully belongs to my ma. I'm guessing she'll get around to inquiring about it when she sees Liling."

And then I turned and sat on my bed. I yawned. It wasn't too hard to look realistic. I was plumb exhausted. Then I lay back down on that dern lumpy cot.

Outside my window, I heard Maude start screechin' to beat the band.

"Let go o' me! Git yer hands off me! Would ye touch yer own ma like that? I didn't think so!"

I resisted a smile. Trying to kill me one day, and tryin' to save my hide the next. Maude sure was an odd duck.

Still, it was a dangerous game she was playing. It was gonna end badly for her no matter what she did. If she took my side, both the sheriff and Liling would make things difficult, if not downright impossible for her to keep breathing.

And when I was gone, either dead or back at the ranch, she was gonna be at the mercy of a world that didn't care much for show people or loud old women.

For some odd reason, I was startin' to get a soft spot for Maude. Even if she suddenly realized she made a mistake and turned around and rode out of town, I'd always hold her in high esteem for thinking of me before her own self. She didn't look a thing like my ma, but right now Maude sure did remind me of her.

"Get back!"

Shhuff-ddduddudd-shuff. That was the sound of someone scuffling with Maude. It was the hard edge of a shoe sole dragging along ridgedy wood. I couldn't picture the sheriff lowering himself to such a level, so it had to be a deputy.

"Unhand me!"

"You can't go in there!"

Bunf! Tee-tuh!

Someone bounced off the thin plank wall that separated the office from the jail. I'm guessing it was the deputy. The body made such an impact that the handle of the heavy lantern on the shelf fell against the wall.

"I'm warnin' you for the last time, woman, stand back or I'll lock you up too."

"Sounds *dee*-vine! A place to sleep, and a meal to boot!"

Silence greeted her declaration. While I was sure the deputy heard the same words from time to time, I guessed he'd never heard them come from a woman's mouth before.

I wondered about Reggie. I supposed he had to stay out of sight for Maude's little charade to work. Everyone knew the Jailer's Son's pa was dead, so if he showed up, everyone would either think Maude was lying or off her rocker.

But something else bothered me. When Liling got wind of my supposed ma comin' to visit me, things were gonna get ugly in a hurry. I truly didn't want anything bad to happen to Maude. She'd had a hard year, probably even more difficult than my year in exile.

The sheriff's low voice reached me from the jail anteroom, but I couldn't make out his words.

A part of me admired his restraint; he could have had her forcibly removed from the building by now. But that was the only thing the sheriff had done that reminded me even a little of my Uncle Turtle. Sheriff Benedict was a bully in a badge. And worse, he was a puppet, and Liling held the strings.

The door suddenly opened.

"Well, ain't this one fine mess ya got yerself into!" Maude said, coming toward me with a smile so sweet and happy I was momentarily taken aback.

I almost had an urge to take a look behind me to see if she was talking to someone else. That's how dern pleased she looked.

"I sure am glad to see you," I said. It was the truth. Even though I knew she wasn't gonna be able to help, it had taken fortitude to see if she could do right by me.

She moved toward me with arms outstretched. I could see by the way she had her thumb tucked into her palm that she had something in her hand.

Whatever it was, it had to be fairly small. It probably wasn't meant to help me get out of jail. It was most likely something sentimental. No matter what it was, it was obvious she didn't want them to see what it was.

She winked. I was intrigued.

I came toward her and stuck my hands through the bars.

"Keep yer hands where I can see 'em!" the sheriff said.

Maude put her arms down, stopped in her tracks and turned back to the sheriff. "A mother can't give her son a hug?"

His nostrils flared. "Might as well. He's gonna hang to-morrow," he said with a shrug.

"Hang?!" she nearly screamed. "What fer?"

When Maude took a step toward the sheriff, I saw him move his hand to the butt of his revolver.

"What? You gonna shoot an old woman? And unarmed, to boot?"

"If you're his ma, you probably don't need a weapon," the sheriff said.

And as Maude took a step back, I heard the soft thud of something small. Then she quickly looked down.

We all did. Maude picked up the small nugget and slipped it inside the top of her dress.

I watched the sheriff's eyes widen. As his lips parted, pre-sumably to ask Maude about the nugget, someone appeared in the doorway behind him.

"I agree," Liling said. "She wouldn't need a gun, if she *were* Maxwell's mother." She pinned Maude with a hate-filled glare. "But you *aren't* his mother, *are* you?"

It truly was so quiet you could hear a pin drop. I think each of us had a reason to keep quiet. Me and Maude didn't want to incriminate ourselves. The sheriff didn't want to appear foolish in Liling's eyes. And Liling wasn't gonna tip her hand when it was much easier to let someone else mess up instead.

"Don't feel bad about bein' confused," I said directly to Liling. "Ye're just plain lucky ye're alive after that explosion."

Maude nodded in agreement. It was almost as if we had rehearsed this moment. She was a surprising woman. There were moments she could look like a dullard, but I guess underneath it all she really was sharp as a tack.

Liling kept cool, but I could tell by the imperceptible narrowing of her eyes that we were gettin' her goat. If it were just one of us contesting her words, she would have had the upper hand. But with two of us, she was outnumbered.

The sheriff turned toward Liling. She kept her eyes trained on me.

"Darlin'?" he asked. "Is there something you'd like to–"

Liling snapped her gaze at Maude. "I will have a word with you outside."

"Why? So you can kill me, too?" Maude shook her head. Her stringy long hair swung wildly. "No, thank ya. I'm jus' gonna stay right here and talk to my son and the sheriff about the situation at hand."

Liling's nostrils flared. "I suggest–"

"This is none of yer business, girl," Maude said, her voice hard. "I suggest you get yer nose outta my business and worry about yer own troubles."

"I will not have you speak to my wife in such a manner!" Sheriff Benedict exclaimed, his spine going ramrod straight.

"Hmmph! And what gives *her* the right to speak to *me* in such a manner?" Maude bandied right back.

He looked totally flummoxed. I was certain he'd never had a woman speak to him in such a manner in the presence of others.

"Where is Reggie?" Liling asked calmly.

"Reggie?" Maude screwed up her face. "You mean that mule that pulled the laundry cart?"

"Your husband." Liling was fairly seething. Her face was composed, but her eyes were glassy. It was an odd combination.

"My husband's dead. You know that."

"Cease this nonsense at once!" Liling commanded, her gaze flicking from Maude to me.

All the while, the sheriff watched with a look akin to shock on his face.

"Nonsense? My son has been wrongly accused of a crime. If I don't intercede, Satan is gonna take my soul when I stop breathing." She slowly shook her head. "I wanna meet my Maker and have Him hold me in His arms when I pass from this earth, not dance in Hell's eternal flames with you."

Maude was a woman of many talents. I couldn't help but be impressed with her acting skills. I rarely underestimated a body, but I truly had with her.

"Arrest her!" Liling told her husband.

"For what?" the sheriff asked, looking uncomfortable. Maybe he did have a spine after all. Or maybe a pinch of conscience hiding somewhere inside him.

The deputy, a stocky man with a thin, graying mustache and beard stepped into the doorway. "Need anything, sheriff?"

"Go away!" Liling commanded.

The man took a hurried step backward and disappeared from sight.

I'll say one thing for Liling. She sure could take command of a situation. And it usually only took just one look or a few words. I'd seen her with Will and how she manipulated him. It wasn't hard to imagine her doin' the same thing to the sheriff, though he wasn't as impressionable as Will.

"I'd have to put her in with...him," he said, pointing to me. "We only got one cell."

"I have eyes," Liling said.

Things at the sheriff's house were gonna be testy tonight, I thought. But Maude looked as alert as a cat watching a mouse. She was thoroughly enjoying Liling's discomfiture.

"And I can't just put a woman behind bars for no –"

"You can and you will!" Liling commanded.

I don't know who was more surprised, Sheriff Benedict, or me. I sure wasn't used to seein' Liling fly off the handle like that. Maybe the explosion really *had* done a bit of rearranging' in that skull of hers. She suddenly seemed wild, like Chester had been, or maybe a bit like a bottle of jigglin' nitroglycerin.

At the sound of hurried footsteps outside the office, I perked up. Rushed steps weren't something you usually heard unless there was trouble brewing. Liling and Sheriff Benedict both turned sharply at the sound of the office door swinging open in a hurry.

A young man raced into the anteroom. I caught a glimpse of him and then he disappeared from sight, but not before I saw the slip of paper in his hand – a telegram.

An irritated look flitted across Liling's face.

"You," the sheriff said to Maude. "Come with me."

Maude shrugged. She knew I'd be all right alone with Liling. Without a word, she followed the sheriff into the front of the building.

Once they were gone, Liling moved a step closer to me, but I noticed she was still out of arm's reach. She smiled then. It was a triumphant smile that didn't make sense to me, unless she was plannin' on shootin' or stabbin' me to death in the next few seconds.

The man's voice rose a bit. I was sure I wasn't supposed to

hear what he said, but I did. And Liling did, too.

"They're on their way," the man said.

Liling's eye narrowed, but she didn't turn toward the office.

"Who?" It was the sheriff's hushed voice.

Liling continued to stare at me, but I could tell all her available senses were trained on the anteroom.

"The Deputy U. S. Marshal. And he's bringing a posse."

My heart flip-flopped at his words. Liling continued to stare at me.

"Why?" Sheriff Benedict asked. "I already have Beck in custody."

"No," the young man said, his voice barely above a whisper. "I don't think Beck is a wanted man no more. They're comin' for your wife."

 Distractions

Liling turned and filed out of the room. The sound of Maude cackling like a wild woman was quickly becoming an irritation to me, but only because it masked the hushed voices of the men.

It was nice to know Liling finally might get a taste of the trouble she'd doled out with such a heavy hand. But she had a way of weaseling out of things that would kill most men, so I didn't put much stock in seeing any type of retribution come to pass.

"Git!" I heard a deputy say, and then the shuffle of Maude's worn-out shoes heading toward the door.

"I'll be back, sonny!" she called.

"See ya, Ma!" I said. "Thanks for stoppin' by!"

The door clicked shut.

The voices of the men were now so low as to be indistinguishable. I heard a word now and again, but knew enough not to try to piece the bits together.

I did hear one thing, though, and it came to me loud and clear:

"Hang him now."

It was Liling's voice.

She needed to have me dead if she was gonna talk her way out of trouble when the Deputy U. S. Marshal came to town. That went for Maude too, and whoever else had ties to me.

Liling was gonna keep killing people if I didn't do something about it. The only good thing I heard was that I wasn't a wanted man. If what I heard was true, I was sure it was all due to the efforts of my Uncle Chase Beck, sheriff of Deadwood.

Even if the U. S. Marshal was coming with a hundred men, he couldn't turn back the hands of time. If I were dead before he got here, it would make things easier for Liling. If Maude and Reggie just happened to wind up dead along with me, there would be no one to question about what had transpired in this not-so-sleepy little town.

If Liling were smart, she'd disappear before they arrived. If I were in her shoes, I would. Even if she looked different than most women, I had no doubt she could pass herself off as anyone, woman or boy even, if she made up that vicious mind of hers.

The only problem with her leaving was that she'd have to take care of loose ends in a big hurry. If she wanted me to hang, it was probably gonna have to happen sooner than later.

And me – I just plain had to find a way out of jail before that hangin' rope found me.

The next sounds I heard were a door opening and slamming shut barely a second apart. I heard the sound of racing hooves next. I sure hoped it was Maude getting' away.

More hurrying footsteps followed, but this time they were on the plank walk in front of the sheriff's office. Most likely they belonged to the man from the telegraph office.

If I were Liling, I would just vamoose. I didn't hear the reason why the Deputy U. S. Marshal was coming to arrest her, but if it was on account of thieving, she might just stay and take her chances. If it was for murder, she'd be better of goin' into hiding.

No matter the reason the posse was on its way, I was

positive my uncle got the ball rolling for Liling's arrest. He was the most logical person to do so.

The door swung open yet again, and Sheriff Benedict entered. He had a cocky look on his face. I glanced behind him. Liling was either gone or waiting on the other side of the wall.

"Well," I said. "I'm waitin'."

His forehead crinkled. "What for?"

"I heard the telegraph man. I ain't wanted no more."

"That's just hearsay."

"It's the truth."

This was gonna go on until hell froze over if I didn't tip my hand.

"Spring me this instant and I won't press charges for wrongful incarceration."

The cocky look faltered but came right back. "You are bold one." He walked near the cell, but not close enough for me to snake a hand out to grab him.

"Not bold. Just expressing my legal rights."

"You don't have any. So things bein' what they are, you're gonna sit tight right where you are."

This was where I knew things were gonna go downhill in a hurry. "And just what are things?" I asked.

"I got a wanted poster saying' you're wanted for murder. You're gonna die in this town, but it's not gonna be by hangin'."

"Is that so?"

Sheriff Benedict nodded. "You're gonna die while trying to escape."

"Well, we both know that ain't gonna happen," I said a little louder than necessary in case the deputy was out there and either had the fear of the Lord running through his veins, or a twinge of conscience left in him. "I ain't guilty, or wanted. And I'm not gonna try to escape."

He looked irritated and not a little taken aback that I

would speak so loudly. I don't know why. To me, it was kinda like expecting a dog you beat to lick your hand.

"If you're gonna kill me to shut me up, you're gonna have to make sure the bullet gets me just so. My uncle knows a detective who can get to the bottom of a ratted up mystery so quick it would make your head spin. And if you try to burn the evidence, it won't do you one bit of good." I smiled then. "He'll go through my burned bones with a fine-tooth comb until finds what he's lookin' for."

I wanted to rattle him a bit and make him think things through before taking rash action. Not sure if I accomplished it because he abruptly turned and walked away.

The next thing I knew, the front door opened and shut. The sheriff had left.

"Anybody there?" I called out a minute later.

I heard the scrape of a chair moving across the floor. It was a reluctant sound. The sound of stiff-soled boots followed.

The deputy with the long mustache entered. He was prematurely gray, but had a baby face with no lines to speak of. I wondered if being entrusted with upholding justice, or having to deal with the sheriff and his evil bride had aged him.

"Whaddya want?" he asked, his glance not meeting mine.

"Are they plannin' on hanging me today, or not?" I asked.

"You sure don't beat around the bush."

"Well?"

He nodded.

"I didn't do anything wrong, you know."

He didn't say anything this time.

"You didn't answer my question, deputy."

He kept his eyes averted. I weighed my options. I could tell him that he'd have blood on his hands if he let me hang when he knew I was innocent and maybe push him the other way. Or I could ask for a favor and give him a better memory of this wretched affair.

"I'm near dyin' of thirst," I told him.

He glanced my way and stared at me for a long time. Apparently, he'd been warned over and over about not giving me an inch because I'd take a mile.

"One cup o' water and you can go back to doin' what you were doin'," I persisted, raising my hands in the air to show him I was harmless.

"Guess I can do that for you," he said, making it sound like I gave him a big list of chores, and he was picking one out.

"I'd be much obliged." I cleared my throat to show him how dry it was.

He went to the corner and poured some water from a big earthenware jug into a tin cup. I always liked the sound of moving water. It was so refreshing and rejuvenating. I kept my expression easy as he approached, but cleared my throat again to cement in his mind that I was thirsty.

"Here you go," he said, holding the cup out to me about three feet away from the cell. The deputy wasn't going to make it easy.

"Wait a minute," he said, withdrawing his hand and the cup of water. "I remember hearing a story about you."

Drat! He'd heard about my scuffle in my uncle's jail when Herrold, a prisoner, had almost gotten the better of me.

"Story?"

"Yeah. I remember it now." He paused and narrowed his eyes. "You're pretty handy with a rope. I bet you're gonna try slipping the noose, ain't ya?"

I was so relieved; I could've laughed out loud. Instead, I sighed. "You ain't gonna say nothin' to the sheriff, are ya?"

"He should know that much hisself," he said after darting a sneaky look behind him.

The deputy stepped closer. I took special care not to glance at his holstered revolver and the set of keys that hung off his belt. Though I didn't see it, I knew he was also carrying a knife strapped to his ankle.

"You're not my buddy, so don't go gettin' any bright ideas," he said as he handed me the tin cup.

It was gonna be close, but if I could grab his wrist, I should be able to set the rest of my plan into motion. Not that I had much of a plan. Most times, I only had an inkling of what would, or should, happen. This was one of those times.

I heard the sound of rushing footsteps again. They belonged to the telegraph man, but I gave no indication that I heard anything.

When the front door opened, the deputy's face crinkled into a mask of guilt. He swung around, his free hand going for his gun.

Sluppp! A slop of water from the cup hit the gritty planks beneath his feet. The lawman, already strung out, dropped his gun and hurriedly bent to scoop it up.

"Sheriff!"

"He's gone," the deputy said, relaxing at what must've been a familiar voice.

I caught a glimpse of a dust-covered young man, clutching a slip of paper. It looked like a telegraph or maybe a note, but it was probably the latter, as the man from the telegraph office had ridden one in just minutes ago.

The insides of me deflated a bit at the realization that my only real chance to escape a lynching was slipping away. I kept a poker face just the same.

The sheriff told me too, that I wasn't gonna die by hanging, that I was gonna die trying to escape, but it was an out and out lie. He was doin' his best to confuse me until they could get a gallows set up or find a sturdy hangin' tree.

The deputy gave me an odd look before placing the cup on a plank shelf and walking away. I sure would've liked to hear what the young man wanted to discuss with the sheriff, but the deputy closed the door tight behind him.

I listened to the low murmur of voices for what couldn't have been more than a few seconds. Then the door of the office opened and closed. The man's steps outside the building were more hurried than the first man who came to see the sheriff with paper in his hand.

Interesting, I thought. It was almost as if the new batch of information was more urgent than the first, and I truly couldn't picture what would be more important than the Deputy U. S. Marshal coming to town with a posse.

When the lawman returned to the jail a minute later, he looked unsettled, as if the news had something to do with him personally.

"You look a little peaked," I said.

"I'd worry more about yer ownself if I were you," he grumped. But then the deputy did the one thing I didn't think he'd do; he gave me a chance to save my neck.

Chapter 9

Escape Into Danger

"Go on. Take it," the deputy said. "I don't have all day."

He handed me the tin cup with the slosh of water that was left in it. If it had been any other time, I probably would have asked him to give me enough water to actually satisfy my thirst, but I wasn't gonna take him from his already distracted state where I had an advantage.

I slowly reached for the cup, but when I was within a few inches of grasping it in my thumb and fingers, I shot my hand out and caught him by the wrist instead.

"Hey–" his yell was cut short as I yanked him tight against the bar of the cell with as much strength as I could muster. The water in the cup splashed up like a tiny fountain, and then slopped at my feet, while the tin cup clanked hard against one of the bars before clattering to the floor.

I simultaneously grabbed the deputy's gun as his shoulder made contact with the bar and jammed it between his shoulder blades. When tried to twist away, I brought the side of his head against an unyielding metal bar. His head made a loud *bmmmk!* sound.

Before he could react, I swung my leg through the bar and brought it back against his leg so he couldn't get away while I lifted his key ring off him. But like everything else that had happened the past day, nothing went my way. One of his keys caught against his pocket and I had to give it an extra yank.

Rrrrrp. His pocket ripped away from his trousers, freeing the key ring. It only took a second to find what I hoped was the right key – there were two of 'em that looked the same – then jammed it inside the keyhole. I twisted but didn't hear the click that told me it was the right key. I flipped the other key to the keyhole and twisted, all the while keeping the stunned deputy clamped against the bars.

Ckkkklkkk. This time the key fit like a hand in a glove. I pushed against the bar, though I had to give it an extra good shove because the deputy's body was providing resistance.

The door creaked outward.

"Stop what ye're doin'!" the deputy said, his words distorted because his face was smushed against the metal bar.

"Sorry, deputy," I said, giving him no liberties. "I know you got a heart under that vest of yers, but no one else in this town does. They're gonna hang me without a trial, and there's not one part of it that spells justice."

"No. You don't under–"

I could've stood there and argued all day, but the way I figured it, I was wasting precious time. The sheriff, Liling, or both might be back any second.

I tossed the revolver into the air by the butt, grabbed it by the barrel and gave the back of the deputy's head a good clunk. I didn't want to kill him. I just wanted him to sleep for a while.

As he slumped to the planks, I gave the door a good heave 'til I was able to slip through. First order of business: find my weapons. My uncle kept things under lock and key in a safe in his office.

I hurried to the door and poked my head into the office – empty. The feeling of being out of that jail cell was like a weight bein' lifted off my chest. It reminded me of when I finally walked away from what was left of the traveling show. Freedom was something I would never take for granted.

The window afforded me a prime view of the main

street. I saw a mother scolding a young boy who stuck his hand into a horse trough directly across the street, but other than that, the streets were mostly empty.

The sound of two pairs of footsteps on the planks toward the end of the raised walk made my heart slow in my chest. Whoever it was had just stepped off the road, up onto the planks. I remembered the layout of the front of the building from when I'd been led here by Liling's henchmen.

Plank walks sound denser at the ends because passersby tend to pause there to chat and also to wait for folks or animals that might be crossing the street. The more steady weight of a body tended to settle the boards and make them more solid. The only other places on a walk that sounded that firm were the areas directly in front of a shop window.

That meant I only had a few seconds to get my belongings and skedaddle before someone either walked past or entered the sheriff's office.

I saw the telegram on the desk and thought to stuff it into my pocket, but every moment counted. First order of business was locating the safe. In Deadwood, the safe was hidden in a secret compartment concealed behind the false front of a secretary desk. It was actually quite clever.

The safe in this office was a simple lock box under the desk that the sheriff and deputy on duty used as a foot stool. It was locked, of course, and though I believed I could open it, I didn't have the time right now. I would have tried the keys on the ring, but I had a sneaking suspicion Benedict was the sole holder of the safe key. In any event, the blades of each of the keys on the ring were too long to fit the safe keyway.

The footsteps were getting closer. Through the shiny glass of the office window, I saw two men in hats pause near the door. They were turned toward the street, as if looking for something or someone, so I didn't get a look at their faces. I doubted they were come to offer me assistance though.

They could be businessmen or well-dressed vigilantes. I knew enough not to assume anything. They might be unarmed collectors of revenue or bank men, though I'd yet to see one wear a cowboy hat like the one I'd started wearing. The footsteps halted at the door. I heard a very low voice which was nearly a whisper:

"Sheriff's gone." I also heard what sounded like, "Wilfred ain't gonna put up much of a struggle."

It was possible I was hearing things, but the fine cracks between the door and the door jamb seemed to provide a telescopic path for the volume of the man's words. Now I was leaning toward the idea that the two men were vigilantes.

The door opened as I ducked behind the desk. From my crouched down position, I could assess the situation. No sense killing someone when I didn't really know what their intention was.

"Wilfred?" a voice somewhat familiar to me called out. The sound of their boots stopped, too. The voice, though, circled through my brain as I fought to remember the owner of the voice.

As I tried to recall the name, I pictured them glancing at each other with wary, uneasy eyes. No one was in the office that they could see. And they undoubtedly knew that I was a prisoner if they were comin' when they knew the sheriff was gone.

"Stay put. I'll look in the jail," said the other man in an agitated voice.

I stayed still as a church mouse. I was gonna have to move soon enough, but if I anticipated a thing too early, or just plain wrong, I'd probably end up with a bunch of bullets in me and never make it back to Deadwood. And right now, I couldn't think of a thing I wanted more than to see Patience's smiling face.

A feeling of urgency enveloped me. The two men were gonna find me eventually. I couldn't stay where I was forever.

The sound of a pair of boots walking past the desk and into the jail made my backbone stiffen, but I didn't move. There was no need for whoever was in those boots to look back at the desk and possibly see me biding my time near the corner.

Oddly, the second man didn't move. If it had been me, I would've wanted to check out the papers on the desk to see if I could find a clue as to why the sheriff's office was in a state of disarray.

"He got away! Wilfred's in here," the man in the jail called back to the office, softly, but in a clearly surprised voice.

They would soon be after me. But strangely, the manner in which he said the words almost sounded like he was glad I got away.

Just as I was steeling myself for shootin' my way out if I had to, I heard:

"Go, Maxwell. Now."

It was just a whisper. And when I heard the words this time, I stuck the name with a body: the voice belonged to my self-professed brother, Raoul.

"I'm comin'," were Raoul's next hushed words to his partner.

The sound of his boots moving toward the jail made me pop my head up from the edge of the desk. Raoul continued ahead without a glance in my direction, so I got to my feet. I watched for a moment to see if this wasn't some sort of trick, though my gut told me it wasn't.

When he disappeared from sight, my glance swept the desk and for a split second I paused when it locked on the telegrams. I thought to pick them up, but they weren't something that would help me and I just might make a noise that would alert the other fella with Raoul and I wasn't sure he wanted the other fella to know I was still inside the sheriff's office.

I wished I had my own guns and belt and the other things the sheriff had taken from me, but right now I was just gonna be happy to escape with my life. I slipped through the half-open door and made my way out onto the boardwalk on nearly soundless well-worn boot soles.

Once outside, I forced myself to keep a slow, unhurried pace, like I was a citizen of this town out for a stroll. I then slipped around the side of the jail. Raoul and whoever else was with him were probably looking out the back.

There was only enough room for a body to fit through the path between the jail and what looked like a barber shop. I say barber shop because while there was a weatherworn pole propped up against the rail in the front, its red, white, and blue helix of stripes were barely recognizable anymore. I didn't see a sign or anything else advertising shaves or baths.

I glanced back over my shoulder and then to the front as I made a quick check of the deputy's revolver to see how many bullets were in the chamber. Then I tucked it into the waistband of my trousers because I had some climbing to do.

"Fetch the sheriff!"

It was a man's voice. It wasn't Raoul's, which I figured was a good thing. But it was the prod I needed to take action. Even though the street looked fairly deserted, any second someone was either gonna come running from the front or the back. That was just how things were in these little towns.

Although I didn't get a good look at the rooftop of the jail on my way into town on account of having a hood over my head 'til I reached the front of the building, I was sure it was a typical slanted roof. Now that I was on the outside of the building, I didn't see any fancy hip or gable ends to tell me different.

I brought the left side of my boot and left palm tight against the building that housed the sheriff's office, and the right side of my boot and my right palm tight against the barber shop building. Then, using my fingertips to steady me, and angling my boots as sharply as I could for traction, I climbed between the walls to the top of the buildings as quickly as I could.

At the top, I twisted over onto the jailhouse roof. I hadn't climbed a building in ages, but I guessed it was a skill one never forgot, because it only took me a few seconds. I knew my thighs would be sore later for my troubles, but right now they were cooperatin' and I was glad.

A nice breeze wafted over me and once again I thought how good it felt to be out from behind bars and in the open. I truly hoped I'd never land in jail again.

The sun was already making its way to its zenith. A bank of thin, wispy clouds was rolling in, but they weren't rain-clouds, so the day was gonna be a fine one. From atop the jailhouse, I had an exceptional view. I even heard the soulful sound of a train whistle, though I couldn't see it.

My glance went east, to where I figured Deadwood lay. It was also gonna be the most traveled route in or out of town, which meant that the potential to run into the U. S. Marshal's posse was just as great as the potential to run into any men who wanted to lynch me.

As I stared east, I saw a tiny dust cloud in the distance. It appeared to be half dozen riders. Could be the Marshal's posse, but it could be almost anything else, too, like the sheriff's thugs, or even a herd of hoofed beasts.

As I crept across the top of surprisingly new shingles to get the lay of the town, I spent a minute thinking about Raoul. I guessed I wasn't as surprised to see him as I was him giving me a helping me a hand by letting me slip out of jail unnoticed.

But then I thought about the coincidence of Liling and Raoul being in the same town. Raoul did go against our evil grandfather and got shot in the back for his troubles, but if he was in the same space as Liling, he almost had to be under her thumb in one way, shape, or form.

Something else in the distance snared my attention. Vultures flying toward town. Two of 'em. The ugly creatures in varying numbers had dogged my steps for last two years, and even though there were only two instead of the trio I had come to know and hate, something told me it was somehow the same vile birds.

I knelt down then and gave the immediate area a closer look. The town was small even by small town standards, but it would make things easy for me to find whatever needed finding. However, it would also make things more difficult to make a clean get-away without a maze of roads to help me.

A couple of horses were tied nearby. One had a sway back and the other looked like it had been run hard already, so I knew they didn't belong to Raoul or his partner. If worse came to worse, though, I'd have to borrow one of 'em. They were better than nothing.

The livery was just down the block in my line of vision. Huàn was waiting, impatiently I was sure, for me to get him out of the tight space he was staying in. I had no doubt he was just as unhappy in a stall as I'd been behind bars. The problem was; the livery would be the first place they'd look for me.

I scooted across the long side of the roof toward the east side of town. The rooftop was already warm, and it sure felt good to have sunshine on me again. My warm feelings were cut short at the sound of a loud whoop and a whinny.

The whoop came out of a man I didn't know, but the whinny came out of Huàn. He was being led out of the livery by Raoul's pal and Huàn, who seemed torn between bolting and bein' happy that he was getting out of his tight quarters. Still, Huàn wasn't making it easy for the man until Raoul grabbed his reins.

Huàn pranced sideways, snorted, and bobbed his head with the spirit of some fine racing horse, but he did seem more at ease now that Raoul had snagged him. Still, I wasn't sure what he was doing. Three horses, two men. It was almost as if they were bringing Huàn right to me.

A trio of cowboys burst out of the saloon down the road on the opposite side of the sheriff's building and ran toward the livery. I kept low, still not sure what was brewin' below me, or what I was gonna do next. The only thing I knew for sure was that I needed to do *something*.

The dust cloud in the distance was getting some volume to it, the vultures were getting closer, and the townspeople apparently were starting to get wind of trouble in this part of town. Most importantly, Huàn might get away from me before I could get my hands on him. There was no hope that I could land on his back even if he did run right past the back of the jailhouse, chances were I'd break his back or my own in the process.

Just as I was about to tip my hand and let 'em know where I was, I heard Raoul yell: "They're heading west!"

All three cowboys pivoted and raced back the way they'd come. If Raoul and his pal were vigilantes, they were good ones. Uncle Turtle always said a vigilante was a vigilante, and that no man had the right to usurp the law, but as time went on, and I found myself bein' hunted for crimes I didn't commit, I disagreed. He saw things in black and white, but sometimes things were gray.

Daaaaay! Daaaaay! I called out, paused, then called out again in that unmistakable blue jay voice: *Doo-lim-pick!*

Both Huàn and Raoul looked in my direction. The other man perked up too, but he kept his glance straight out in front of him.

When Raoul spotted me, he swung up in his saddle, keeping a tight hold on Huàn's reins. The other man hurried onto his horse too. So they *were* there to help me.

I picked my way down to the bottom of the roof where I figured I could safely jump, and then land on the ground without damaging my knees or hips. I gave Liling and Sheriff

Benedict a thought just as I heard the unmistakable sound of metal against metal. That could only mean one thing: a bullet was gonna be headed somewhere real quick.

I tried to take in the area to my front and sides as I dropped off the roof, but I couldn't pinpoint the gunman. I caught the first of two bullets in my boot as I left the roof. I felt the buzzy vibration of it all the way through to my leg. Luckily, it only skinned my boot and didn't catch any skin. Apparently whoever was shooting was anticipating what I was gonna do. I was happy their aim was off. The other bullet went through the jailhouse wall.

Huàn whinnied again as I landed on the ground. I was on up on my feet in an instant.

Crr-winnnng! A pause, then: *Ka-pow! Ka-pow!*

Once I had the deputy's revolver out of my trousers, I tried to figure out where all the shootin' was coming from, and raced toward Huàn all at the same time.

It was then that I saw Liling, standing at the side of the livery holding a rifle. I immediately recognized it as a Winchester Model 1873. The .44 looked huge in her hands, though she had a confident stance and the crescent steel-capped butt rested firmly and easily against her tiny shoulder. When she shifted, it was with effortless grace. It appeared as though she fired the weapon ten times every day.

Then she swung it up in my direction.

Chapter 10

The Devil's Right Hand

Even from where I stood, I saw the determined set of her jaw as I aimed, but it turned out she wasn't gettin' a bead on me. She was gonna shoot Raoul in the back, just like his own grandfather had done a year ago.

"Raoul! Down!" I hollered as I fired at her. I never liked shootin' from the hip, but I didn't have no choice, so I just did my best.

I squeezed off a shot at the same time Raoul bobbed his head. I was counting on him doing as I said, otherwise things weren't gonna turn out good for any of us.

Everything at that moment in time seemed to slow down enough for me to take in things as they happened. As Raoul bobbed, he created a clear path from me to Liling. Huàn tore away from Raoul and swung his sleek head in my direction. The cowboys that Raoul had sent in a different direction were now in the street, reaching for their weapons.

Liling was a small target, so I aimed for her chest because it was a bigger area. Luckily, she was so intent on paying Raoul back for betraying her that she kept her attention squarely on him and not me.

Once I had the sight lined up with Liling's black heart, I squeezed the trigger.

I got her. Or someone else did. I guess I'll never know for sure. Her body shot up off the ground with a sideways twist to it. She seemed to recover her balance a tad before she tipped over backward.

Huàn, still racing toward me, was only yards away. I had one chance to hop off the ground and up onto his back. There was too much noise to hear shots being squeezed off, so I focused all my energy on getting on my horse and away from any bullets that might be trying to find me.

I brought my finger away from the trigger as I readied to hop astride Huàn. No sense shootin' myself or someone else during what would surely be an awkward moment. Calculating his stride, I waited until Huàn was a step behind me, then grabbed his loose rein and swung up when his rear hooves pushed off the road like we'd practiced a hundred times.

Once on his back, I spun in the other direction and felt my blood run cold. Just that quick, Liling had picked herself up off the ground!

I had a silly thought then, but it was one I couldn't stop. Maybe I couldn't kill Liling no matter what I did because she couldn't be killed.

Raoul and his partner stayed low in their saddles. Neither of 'em paused for me, bullets, or anything else. They just kept riding out of town, in a southerly direction.

Me and Huàn caught up to them in short order. Once I gathered the reins in my hand and saw that Raoul and the other man didn't have anything sneaky up their sleeves, I looked back. A couple cowboys were behind us.

This was a bit new to me. I was usually the one trailing somebody else, not the other way around. One of us three in the front was probably gonna get hit. And if one of the cowboys got wild with their bullets in their zeal to make a name for himself, a horse could go down too. It would be a shame, because each of us was atop a fine mount.

Once we hit a forked trail, I hollered, "Split up!"

Immediately, Raoul's friend veered left. Raoul continued straight, and I veered right. As it stood, one or two of us could make a clean getaway. Whoever was left would have to deal with whatever mess followed.

An occasional bullet zinged past me, which meant the two were gonna follow me. Huàn stuck out like a sore thumb, and for once I was glad. Raoul and his friend had done me a favor. I didn't want them to have to keep dodging bullets.

Every once in a while I heard a shot, but they weren't stupid. They would save the ammunition until they closed the distance between us, or could get a clean shot at me.

They were playing it smart because they saw how Huàn could run. Horses like Huàn didn't come along very often, so when they took care of me, they were gonna take possession of Huàn. Picturin' them trying to turn my horse's allegiance made me smile despite the direness of the situation.

A series of deep rolling hills lay ahead of me. It would mean slowing down, but it would also give me a chance to ditch the riders behind me. Huàn was at his best when I gave him his head in hilly country. I even told Hinto once that Huàn must have part mountain goat in him because he could darned near climb the side of the cliff, and with me on top of him, to boot.

Then, the oddest thing happened. It truly had a dream-like feel to it. Indians appeared and it made me wonder if Hinto had anything to do with it. There were two in one group and three in another, but Hinto wasn't one of 'em. The two groups of Indians were about a hundred yards apart.

What were they doin' here? Worse yet, how was I gonna make it past 'em before the cowboys caught up to me?

Huàn kept running, heedless of any potential danger and I didn't do a thing to stop him. The sounds of his hooves hitting the ground and big heaves of air escaping his lungs as he did his best for me were loud in my ears.

And then a curious thing happened. An Indian in one group and an Indian in the other shifted their weapons so they were parallel with their bodies.

They were allowing me to pass through!

"Yee-ah!" I urged Huàn even though he didn't need any prodding. I knew without looking that the cowboys were still a good distance behind me because they'd stopped shooting. Even an idiot knew enough not to waste good bullets on foolishness.

As I reached the two groups of braves, they began to come together. I raised my hand in thanks as I passed by and then looked over my shoulder.

The cowboys were still coming, but they suddenly slowed. Riding into a group of Indians was way worse than being ambushed. If the two cowboys had any sense at all, they would know they were outnumbered and outwitted.

The moment I passed through, the braves with the lances moved the pointed ends of them toward each other, effectively showing the cowboys that they should stop and turn around. If they didn't, they would die for their troubles. Hinto wasn't among the braves, but I knew in my gut he had something to do with them bein' here.

I kept a keen glance ahead of me and to my sides. I didn't see Raoul or the other man, but I didn't expect to. The only thought I gave them was a flitting one: they were vigilantes. Except in this case, Raoul and his riding partner were vigilantes who did bad things to make things right. Not the other way around.

Although Raoul had been part of the traveling show, and was raised with a dubious set of morals to wrestle with, his moral self seemed to have broken free. I was glad he survived the bullet our grandfather had pumped into his back.

Still, I had no idea how Raoul knew enough to come to that wretched town to find me, though I just knew his knowledge was linked to Liling.

I gave Huàn's neck a pat, looked back over my shoulder and leaned back in the saddle to let Huàn know we could slow things down a bit. No sense wearing' us both down. A man just never knew when his wherewithal was gonna be needed down the line.

The dust cloud I tracked coming into town was most likely the U. S. Deputy Marshal and the men he'd deputized. If it was, what was Liling doing, hanging around town when she could be on her way to Mexico? It didn't make sense.

Just ahead of us, a little pond at the bottom of two hills looked like just the place to rest and get a drink. Things would probably seem clearer once my frazzled brain had a chance to sort through them.

After me and Huàn sated our thirst, I looked all around. I wasn't too keen on being at the bottom of the hill for any length of time, but this was as good a place as any to pause for a few minutes.

After rechecking the chamber of Deputy Wilfred's revolver again, I reached inside my secret pocket and fingered the locket I'd given Patience, and the little braid of her hair. While it was a comfort to touch her personal items, something niggled at me.

She had to be in some sort of danger. Just the fact that I was holding something that she always had hangin' around her neck didn't bode well for her health. And the hair ... I didn't like to think about how someone took possession of something so personal.

A strong feeling that she wasn't the only one in danger made me pop my head toward town at the exact moment Huàn gave a warning whinny.

I drew my revolver with an upward angle. It wasn't entirely uncomfortable, but it did give my arm added weight to deal with.

The man in my sights wasn't entirely unexpected, either: Raoul. And he had his hands in the air.

"It's me," he said as he rode closer.

That little voice in the back of my head that sometimes told me something wasn't quite right started squawking. Without being too obvious, I took in as much of the hills around me as I could without turning my head. Then, in the periphery of my vision, I caught sight of another man on a horse.

"What do you want?" I asked.

"You don't sound all that happy to see me," Raoul said, sounding thoroughly offended. "I want to help you."

Then the man Raoul was riding with appeared a short distance away. Something about the way they were spread out told me they wanted to make sure I wasn't goin' nowhere.

Now I knew how cattle felt when we rounded 'em up. I heard the sound of blood pumping in my ears and reminded myself to stay calm.

"Can't help me from up there," I said, nodding my head at the other man.

Raoul chuckled then, and it was a genuine sound. I felt myself relax a bit. Maybe livin' in exile had made me too paranoid and fidgety for my own good.

"I'm coming down now. Ambrose, too. Keep your finger off the trigger, Max," he said. His voice sounded different than mine, a little more refined than I remembered.

Raoul and his partner picked their way down the slope to the spring-fed pond near me. They drank alongside their horses, wiped their faces with fine cloth bandanas and made their way over to me when they were finished.

I hadn't seen Raoul in a year. Time had been kind to him. He had a nice haircut and a citified look to him. Ambrose, in his late twenties or early thirties I guessed, also had a look about him that suggested he didn't do his own wash or cooking.

"Pretty nice o' you both to risk yer necks to save mine," I said.

The man named Ambrose lifted an eyebrow, but didn't say a word. Probably thought I was an ingrate. I heard the sarcasm in my voice with my own ears.

"Well, *brother*," Raoul said, reminding me of our bond.

"I'm sure you'd do the same for me. And since Ambrose is a friend of mine, he thought he'd come along for the ride."

I inclined my head but still wasn't ready to thank 'em with words. Too much needed answering.

"How'd you come to be in the same town as Liling?" I asked. Raoul and Liling had to have some sort of connection. And any connection, tenuous or not, couldn't be good.

"I could ask you the same thing." The lower half of Raoul's nicely shaved face turned downward. "As for me, I will answer that with two words. You can take your pick of fate or chance." He gave me a look from the top of my head to the tips of my boots. "I'm still not sure which. Maybe there is no difference."

"What's yer profession?" I asked Raoul, but nodded at Ambrose, too.

"I own the Dragon Saloon. Ambrose is my manager."

My brain substituted the word *accomplice* for manager.

I did some calculating. In the space of a year, Raoul had accomplished what it took other men decades to do? And with what means? The gold from our grandfather's coffers was nowhere near enough to fund that sort of enterprise.

"You've done well for yerself," I told him.

He didn't say anything, though his lips took on a sour twist. The conversation was going downhill fast, but I'd rather fight with words than bullets. The trouble was, I wasn't exactly a wordsmith.

"So tell me, Raoul, why would a rich man risk his neck to help a man he barely knew?"

Raoul's face tightened in annoyance. "I was attempting to return a favor. Now you're making me reconsider my well-intentioned actions."

"I do thank you," I said, again inclining my head to include Ambrose. "And I apologize," I said, swallowing my pride. "It hasn't been an easy year."

He made no mention of my understatement and took in

the area around us, much as I had. Ambrose, too, kept his eyes peeled.

A distant gunshot could be heard, then silence followed.

"As for Liling," Raoul continued, "she's a thorn in my side. She found me here and then planted herself in town. I tried to find a reason to send her on her way, but she won't budge. If anything, she put down even deeper roots. However, for the most part, she leaves me to my own devices."

His words made me feel a little better because they were logical. But if I were in his shoes, I would have crossed the ocean twice to get away from her.

"She's not right in the head," he said.

"Has she ever been?" I asked.

He smiled, revealing teeth much like mine. He wasn't wearing a suit, but his clothes were fine and he had a nice shave. He was a man of means, not a man pretending to be a man of means. In the space of a year Raoul had become a proprietor, while I had spent the same time dodging bullets and evading the law.

I was never one to ponder the fairness of a situation, but this was one time I allowed myself to feel the sting of it. But only for a moment. Then I put it out of my head.

"I heard she sustained damage to an arm and a leg," I said. "It's rumored she wears a metal plate over her chest as some sort of armor."

"You've been in town for a day, and already you know what it took me months to learn," Ambrose said. His brow lifted in amusement.

The fact that my words might have some truth to them was a revelation to me however. The bullet that struck Liling when I was making my getaway must have been deflected by the rumored metal plate. Otherwise, how could a body that slight get back up again after taking a direct hit?

Sarge was pretty close-mouthed about bein' in the war, but he did say he got shot and that his sword had taken a bullet. He said it probably saved him from getting his leg amputated. And my Uncle Turtle said his badge saved his life. He even showed it to me. The metal was dented so badly I was amazed it hadn't broken one of his ribs.

But Liling was married. I couldn't picture a man being agreeable with his own wife wearing a piece of metal across the front of her.

Moving my glance to Raoul, I said, "She tried to shoot you in the back."

"Well, there you have it," he said, sounding much like Will.

There was an easiness about my self-proclaimed brother that I almost envied.

"Believe me when I say I owe you my life, Max. I have no ulterior motives."

And that was the end of me wondering about Raoul.

Ambrose wiped his face with his bandana again, then slipped his hand inside his fancy vest to retrieve something or other. As he fumbled about, I saw the edge of a folded sheet of paper. It was a telegram.

Before I knew it, I brought out my Colt.

"Hands in the air."

Raoul and Ambrose both complied, though I only meant Ambrose. Raoul didn't hide his look of irritation.

"What now, Maxwell?" Raoul asked.

"Why don't you tell me?"

"I would if I had a clue what you were talking about."

"The telegram in Ambrose's vest pocket."

"Ambrose, please take out the telegrams you took from the good sheriff's office. I'd like to take a closer look at them myself."

Ambrose did as Raoul asked. First he showed me his hands again, much like a magician would show an audience, then unbuttoned that fine vest of his and pulled out several folded notes.

"You're welcome to read them aloud," Ambrose said, handing them to me. "That is, if you can read."

I ignored his little jab and took a few steps back. While I did so, I took in the hills. No one had joined us. Not yet, anyway.

The first telegram said in one sentence that the U.S. Deputy Marshal would arrive in Plankville on Wednesday, accompanied by deputies, to take Liling, a Chinese woman, into custody. I didn't read it aloud. I was surprised the sheriff had left it behind.

After reading it, I took in the two men with their hands still up, and read the second telegram. As I began, my heart stopped. The words were simple: *Sheriff Chase Beck en route to Plankville.*

The importance of the second telegram hit me like a brick upside the head. If my uncle was en route, he knew I was in town. And when he arrived, Liling would kill him. I was fleeing the very town I needed to remain in.

"Well?" Raoul looked genuinely curious.

"I guess I need to go back to town."

Neither shuttered their surprise.

"Go back?" Ambrose asked. "We just fetched you away."

"I already had myself loose," I reminded him. I had no doubt I would've gotten away left to my own devices, but the two of them getting Huàn out of the livery did help me some.

"It bears repeating that you do have a price on your head, Maxwell," Raoul reminded me.

A look of surprise flitted across Ambrose's face. I found it peculiar.

"The U. S. Deputy Marshal is on his way to town right now with a posse. I'm sure when he takes Liling into custody, things will sort themselves out." I paused. "You comin' with me and puttin' in a word or two on my behalf would go a long way to help speed up the process."

Raoul gave me a look and moved his lips into a small sneer. In that moment, he looked the very picture of a wealthy proprietor. But I still didn't know what he was getting at until he asked:

"Do you honestly believe Liling will comply with the law?"

Who really knew what kind of plots and plans ran through that noggin' of hers? I guess I figured she didn't have a choice, unless she wanted to end up with a bullet in her.

"Even if she does ride away with the U. S. Deputy Marshall, you know as well as I do that the posse isn't going to make it back to wherever it came from. At least in the same numbers."

Again, I saw a flicker of alarm in Ambrose's eyes. Odd. Surely he must have heard stories about Liling. If not from Raoul, then from drifters or people who'd had dealings with her.

Liling was evil, but she couldn't kill or pay off everyone who crossed her path. There were people like me, and now Maude and Reggie, who would talk if someone asked questions.

"So what're yer plans?" I asked Raoul. "You gonna lay low 'til Liling's gone? She saw you and Ambrose ride out of town with me. If that ain't reason to kill you, I don't know what is."

"Can I put my hands down now?"

I nodded.

"Yes," he said. "That's my plan."

"But you didn't know about the U. S. Marshal coming to town until I just told you," I said.

He shook his head. His hair caught the sun and became shiny as a raven's wing. Made me wish I could have a bath. I was feelin' pretty dusty.

"Not true. It's a small town, brother. News travels fast."

This time Ambrose's surprise came in the form of a gasp. "That's the second time you've called him brother."

86

"Because he is my brother," Raoul said.

"I thought you used the word, brother, as a term of..." Ambrose glanced between the two of us. "I don't know why I didn't see it before."

"Would it have made a difference?" I asked, not understanding why he was getting all fidgety.

Ambrose glanced back toward town with a nervous look on his puss. "If I would've known you were kin, I wouldn't have–"

"What?" Raoul asked. He looked more angry than perplexed.

"I'm the one who sent the telegram sayin' the U. S. Marshal was comin' to town."

Patience Gone

"Hold on one cotton pickin' minute," I said. "Why would you do such a thing?"

Raoul's hand moved toward his gun. He wasn't gonna shoot his manager, was he? Or was he only letting me think it? Things were as snarled as a girlie's hair on a windy day.

"I didn't want to, I truly didn't!" Ambrose protested. Sweat began to bead on his forehead. "She said she'd kill my intended if I didn't." He rushed ahead, his hands gesturing wildly as he talked. "She left me no choice. I'm sorry, Raoul."

That was one saying I always had a hard time accepting. *She left me no choice.* Far as I was concerned, she gave him two choices, did as she told him, or follow his conscience. Ambrose just decided it was easier to do as she said.

"I can't believe you'd stab me in the back after all I've done for you," Raoul said.

It was obvious that the betrayal hurt. But was Ambrose any different than Raoul had been when he was part of the traveling show?

"You could have come to me. You could have told me," Raoul told Ambrose.

Standing around jawing about something that couldn't be undone was a waste of time as far as I was concerned.

"I didn't know she was gonna try to kill you," Ambrose said. "I swear on the Bible, I didn't know."

Ambrose saying he sent the silly telegram about Liling,

still didn't explain why he sent the one about my uncle coming to town.

"Why did you send the telegram about my uncle coming to Plankville?"

"Your uncle?" Ambrose looked genuinely perplexed. "I only sent the telegram Liling instructed me to send, the one about the U. S. Marshal coming to town to take her into custody."

His words explained why the two telegrams looked so different. One was typed, the other was handwritten.

"Now what?" Raoul asked me, all business again.

"They're gonna ambush my uncle. And if they take him alive, they're gonna torture him until I show my face. The longer I wait, the worse it's gonna be."

"I want to help any way I can," Ambrose said. "I know you think me weak now, and probably don't trust me, but I was only thinking of Edwina. I sincerely want to make amends."

I nodded. There was a little part of me that probably would have thought to do the same thing.

Ambrose started talking again. He sure must've felt bad about what had happened:

"I probably wouldn't have agreed to send the telegram, even with all her threats, but after I saw a picture of what she did to that pretty blonde girl from Deadwood, I was truly afraid for Edwina."

Ma used to say that coincidences were usually anything but a coincidence. My brain told me it was Patience. And even though there were a number of blonde girls in Deadwood, I doubted any of them had spoken to Liling.

"I have a cabinet photo of the girl. Liling told me to keep it with me to remind me what would happen to Edwina if I didn't carry out her wishes."

I felt Raoul's glance on me as I waited for Ambrose to

produce the photograph. Even if he didn't have the same perception of things as I did, I knew he was secretly sweet on Patience, and didn't want any harm to come to her any more than I did.

He reached into the vest pocket on his other side and pulled out the small photo. It was covered with glass and had a thin copper frame. I was sure it had been cut down because photographers rarely took such small images.

Ambrose's hands shook as he handed it to me. I was pretty sure he thought I would be pistol-whipping him at some point.

The first thing I noticed was that the glass had cracked in two. The thin copper around the edges kept it from falling out completely.

"Do you know her?" he asked.

"Maxwell?" It was Raoul this time.

But I didn't trust myself to answer. My heart was pounding so hard in my ears I could barely hear. The face on the photograph was bruised and battered. The young girl's eyes were closed. She might have been resting, but I suspected she was unconscious.

The girl's hair was tied up in an elaborate Oriental twist. It would have been beautiful under any other circumstances. Even the dress on the girl was Oriental. It did little to hide the generous swell of the girl's breasts beneath the silk fabric.

"It's Patience all right," I said, tucking the photo into my pocket. I turned to Ambrose. "The girl I'm gonna marry."

"Dear God!" Ambrose quickly made a sign of the cross over himself with fingers so shaky I thought he was gonna take one of his eyes out.

"Maxwell. You mustn't do anything rash," Raoul said, sounding more like my Uncle Turtle, or my pa, had he been alive.

"I'm gonna end her worthless hide." I couldn't get the battered image of my beautiful, spunky Patience out of my head. It would slowly drive me mad if I let it get the better of me.

"I will help you, brother," Raoul said. He moved his hand toward me.

I shook it. Even if we weren't blood brothers, he would be my brother 'til the day I died. Just like Will. But unlike Will, I knew Raoul would die for Patience. He had a soft spot for her in his heart, although he would never betray me.

Ambrose tentatively offered his hand. "I'd like to try to undo the damage I've done. If you'll allow me."

There was no way to undo any damage as far as I could tell, but he meant well. And if it helped him sleep at night and made him appreciate the woman he was gonna marry, I wasn't gonna deny him the opportunity.

When I nodded and gave his hand a pump, a look of relief flooded his face. I felt better knowing I had two men backing me up, should I need it.

"Much as I'd like to tell you that we need to ride into town and kill Liling, that seems like the last thing we should do," I said.

"What, then?" Raoul asked.

"My uncle is probably already in town. I have a feeling he brought men from the ranch with him, friends of mine." I tried not to think of any of them losing their lives because of me, but it was hard not to when the vision of Liling standing in front of a dead body kept coming to the fore of my thoughts.

"When I was on the roof, I saw a big dust cloud. I thought it might be the U. S. Marshal, but now I'm thinking it's my uncle." I gave Raoul a look. "Your uncle, too."

His eyes widened a bit as he considered it.

"He and his men are looking for me, but Liling is looking for trouble. Lives are gonna be lost." I looked each of them square in the eyes.

"Neither of you have to stand with me. This is my battle,

and mine alone."

"I wish to join you, brother."

"Me too," Ambrose said. He seemed to have perked up a bit at the process of avenging his honor.

"I have a feeling that Liling's father will be riding with my uncle. I sure hope he is, anyway."

Both men looked taken aback by the information.

"Jaw-Long is like a father to me. He warned me about Liling. I'd appreciate it if you'd refrain from doin' him harm, along with anyone riding with my uncle."

I didn't tell them that Jaw-Long was more capable of looking after himself than the two of them put together, but a year had passed. Maybe Jaw-Long's constitution had suffered in the interim.

Both men nodded and Ambrose went to his horse. Raoul turned away from me. He suddenly looked uncomfortable, and I wasn't sure why.

"I own a saloon," he said.

"That's what you said." I wasn't sure what he was getting at. Maybe he was worried about someone burning the place down in his absence, or losing business because he was siding with me.

He looked away. "I employ women."

Again, I didn't see what that had to do with me.

"Women who enjoy the company of men who aren't their husbands."

He had my full attention now. That was one part of the entertainment business I didn't care for. Making money off a woman's misfortune was akin to slavery as far as I was concerned.

"What're ye gettin' at?"

"I'm saying that Patience is dressed like a show girl."

I felt my stomach twist. He was putting words to my worst fears.

"I'm not saying she is, but..." He trailed off. What he didn't say was more powerful than any words he could have used.

"Patience would never–"

"Willingly," Raoul said, his face tight. "But if she..." He seemed to search for the right words. "If she's been compromised, she won't be the same girl you knew in Deadwood."

I didn't doubt his words. I guess I just didn't understand what he was gettin' at.

"If Liling has her working somewhere, she's most likely soiled."

Before I could stop myself, I punched him in the face. I couldn't think of one word I wanted to say to him. I just wanted to punch him again. And again. And again. But what he said was the truth.

Not trusting myself, I took a step back. I heard the sound of my labored breathing in my own ears. It was a strange sound. I couldn't recall ever being so angry. And I was over something that wasn't even Raoul's fault.

"I should have tried to phrase my words more delicately. For that, I apologize," Raoul said, wiping the bloodied corner of his mouth.

I swallowed my rage and accepted the truth of his words, but yet I couldn't say anything. Ambrose had turned to look at us now, so I got my feelings under control as best I could.

"You must know, brother, I'm only telling you this so you know exactly what you're going to come face to face with." He said his words so softly, I didn't worry about Ambrose overhearing. Truth was, I barely heard them myself.

"I want you to know that should you find Patience...unacceptable in any way, you don't have to keep any promise you made."

I never heard such a strange way of wording something. He was talking in riddles without even asking a single question.

"What are you tryin' to say?"

"I fell in love with Patience the moment I laid eyes on her. If you don't want her after what she's been through, I would not think ill of you." He paused. "And know too, that I would ask her to be my wife, and would treat her like a queen until her dying day."

Raoul gave me a piercing look. "You know as well as I do that if you choose to be with Patience, life will never be easy for her in your shadow. You have a reputation to uphold. I am but a businessman."

Chapter 12

Seething

You have a reputation to uphold.

His words made me almost as angry as what he said about Patience. Yet, Raoul had a point. Life with would never be easy for her if she chose to be with me.

The three of us rode back to Plankville, keeping a wary eye all around. The Indians had disappeared, not that I expected them to stick around, and we didn't see another soul.

I didn't look at Raoul once after the last words he spoke to me. My insides were all shook up and the thoughts swirling around in my noggin' weren't no better. I didn't know how I was supposed to feel. Angry? Relieved? Disgusted?

I loved Patience. What I felt for her was a matter of the heart and not some twisted sense of duty. I remembered the feel of her soft pink lips on mine, and with the happy thought, put her to the back of my mind so I could focus on what would surely be a tryin' time.

Once we had Plankville in sight, I motioned to Ambrose, and we split up. Raoul gave me a pointed look and a nod before he rode east. I knew it was his way of trying to make things right, and it was fine by me. A man should never ride with bad feelings in his craw.

I sure hoped Ambrose could take care of himself. In a way, riding back into town might be more dangerous for Raoul and Ambrose 'til things could get sorted out.

My Uncle Turtle and the rest of the men he brought with

him had already exchanged words with Sheriff Buford Benedict. There was part of me that wished I could've been witness to their initial meeting.

Being a sheriff was never an easy thing, especially in the West, but Turtle wasn't the sort to compromise his integrity, or back down from injustice, no matter how great. And while I had no doubt Sheriff Benedict started off the same way, he'd let Liling and her feminine wiles sway him from his duties as a lawman.

As the shining flat roofs of the town came into view, I gave Huàn's neck a pat. "We got work to do, Huàn."

Raoul and Ambrose would most likely meet up with my uncle first. It was probably wishful thinking to believe they could nip any trouble in the bud. Still, I figured the two of them lived in town, so they had the advantage of knowing where things were and what could be accomplished.

I felt fairly sure of my aim with the deputy's revolver, but it still wasn't the same as firing my own gun. My uncle always said shootin' somebody else's gun was like bein' dressed in your Sunday best while takin' cattle to market. It could be done, but you didn't feel comfortable doin' it.

Still, as I rode into the unknown, dread churned my stomach. I pictured a rainstorm of blood, and in the middle of it, my face covered in red. Or was it Raoul's?

Ka-pow pow pow pow!

I didn't need to urge Huàn forward; he muscled toward the gateway of the small town as if he had suddenly sprouted wings.

Crackkkk! Pow! Ka-pow! A pause followed, then so many shots I couldn't count them.

Me and Huàn raced through Plankville's entrance, this time with no sentinels there to intercept us. The sheriff's office was a few blocks ahead. I planned to ride straight to the middle of town, but then I saw Maude, standing smack dab in the middle of the street.

She had her hands in front of her and was shaking 'em like they were on fire. I saw Reggie at her feet.

Ahead of her, men raced across the street. I saw one man atop a roof on the side opposite the sheriff's office. A rider-less horse charged toward me and kept going. I was already into the thick of things.

I spotted what looked like Sarge waddling toward the sheriff's office! That was my first big surprise. The second would come a few seconds later.

"Max! Maxwell!" Maude cried out to me.

I had work to do, but I couldn't leave a defenseless woman in the middle of the street. She'd get killed herself.

Men were darting about like roaches from place to place. None of 'em seemed to notice me, so I reined Huàn up short, a yard or two from Reggie's body.

"She killed 'im!" Maude moaned, her cheeks oddly deflated and her eyes afloat with tears.

"I'll git 'er, Maude," I said, my eyes taking in everything as best I could. Stopping here was tempting fate, but I just couldn't go past. She'd risked her own neck for me. I owed her at least that much.

Reggie was on his side. Tears were leaking from his staring eyes, and I knew he wasn't dead yet, though he would be shortly. The wound was too big to survive.

"She done it!" Maude said. "She lied the whole time and then she shot him anyway!" She wailed again, making my blood curdle at the high pitch of it. "The bitch smiled when she done it, too!"

Something caught my eye. It was Liling, and she was comin' straight for us. I didn't see a weapon on her, but it didn't mean she didn't have one on her.

"Bitch!" Maude screamed, and quick as lightning, Maude wrested my revolver away and fired at her before I knew what happened.

Though I'd practiced shootin' more during the past year of my exile than the rest of my life combined, I was beginning to wonder if I was just plain losing my skills. I'd never had anyone, man or woman, unarm me so deftly without me wantin' 'em to.

My shock was usurped by the thought that, despite my own desire to crush the breath out of Liling with my bare hands, I needed to keep her alive long enough to force the whereabouts of my beloved Patience out of her.

In Maude's haste to do away with her adversary, she tripped over Reggie's arm and fell forward, landing on her face in the road. Her gun immediately discharged, sending Huàn skittering away from the noise.

I kept my eyes peeled for anyone tryin' to get a bead on me while I dove for my revolver. Maude apparently had the same thought. While we wrestled for control, Liling started running. It was one of the oddest things I'd ever seen in my life.

The last time I'd seen her perform, she'd been light as a feather, bending back upon herself like some pocket knife. Today however, there was something almost mechanical about the way she moved. Maybe it was that sheet of metal Raoul said she'd taken to wearing for protection.

"Maude! Let go!" I yelled. I knew it was disrespectful, but she was gonna get us both killed.

Instantly she rolled away so I could get a firing hold on the revolver. It wasn't soon enough.

Liling produced a handgun from her sleeve and whipped it up in front of her. My heart sank when I saw where she was aiming.

"No!" I shouted as we simultaneously fired.

Poh poh poh!

Two of Liling's three shots hit Huàn's broad chest. The other bullet hit him in the neck. A spray of blood rained over me as he issued a throaty wail of pain.

Although I wanted Liling alive so I could force Patience's whereabouts out of her, I also wanted to kill her in the awfulest way possible for taking my best friend from me.

I brought the nose of my revolver up and was about to squeeze off a shot that I hoped would wipe the sneer off her face, when the loud crack of a gunshot sliced the air. Liling tipped over, face first into the dirt, her weapon slipping from her hand like it had grease on it.

The bullet that got Liling sounded like it hit metal, so I guess that meant Raoul was right. Not that the armor had done her any good in the end.

I spun around at the sound of Huàn's loud whinny and high-pitched squeal. He was calling to me one last time.

"I'll get her gun," Maude said, her face solemn.

For a few seconds, as I met my dying friend's eyes, I truly wouldn'ta cared if someone had put a bullet in my head and ended my life. I felt wretched when Ma and Pa expired, but they were each other's best friend. Huàn had been my constant companion for the better part of two years. Now I understood what it felt like to have a body you cared about more than your own hide.

I scuttled over to Huàn, wiping his blood off the end of my nose. He was writhing around a bit, trying to get up. I heard the gurgle of blood in his throat and saw a foamy stream of it shoot from the side of his mouth, but he never stopped moving.

He was doing his best to get up so he could finish what he started – getting me where I wanted to go. His front hooves dragged across the earth, and his eyes rolled wildly as he struggled to keep breathing.

Then he huffed and kinda bawled a little. I thought my heart was gonna burst out of my chest. He had to be hurtin' something fierce, but he still kept trying to get to his feet.

"Hey, boy..." I swallowed the lump in my throat as I assessed his injuries. "Just rest awhile." I ran my hand down his forehead. Blood sprayed out of his nose in a thin mist now too.

The bullet holes looked huge up close, especially the one in his neck, and I truly was amazed he was still breathin'.

"The bitch is dead."

It was Maude's voice, but it sounded like it was a mile away. So did the shootin'.

Huàn struggle again to get up, legs flailing, nostrils flaring and sending a misty plume of blood over my arm.

"You shouldn'ta left yerself open like that, brother," I told him, my breath catching in my throat. "You know better 'n that."

Huàn whinnied and tossed his head. I held on to him, stroking his head while he snorted and gulped in air. His breaths were shallower now, though he continued to struggle to get to his feet.

"You gotta put him out of his misery, sonny," Maude said, her voice soft.

I didn't trust myself to speak right then, so I just nodded. The sounds of sporadic gunfire sounded like they were coming from New York instead of a stone's throw away.

"Thank you, Huàn." It was all I could manage, but it pretty much summed up what I needed to tell him.

My friend bobbed his head as if in agreement, then settled it down one last time on my lap. I brought out the deputy's revolver and placed it against his skull.

He huffed again and rolled his big blue eye up toward me as if to get one last picture of me in his brain.

I turned my head and squeezed the trigger. I flinched at the loud sound of the bullet. Instantly he stilled.

Once I eased myself out from under his head, I got to my feet.

"Sorry, boy. I know you loved that horse," Maude said.

She was a compassionate one, beneath all the grime.

Here she was offering me her condolences when her own man lay dead not a few yards away.

I nodded, smoothly reloaded my revolver and walked over to where Liling lay.

A gentle breeze ruffled the hem of her fine dress, exposing a layer of white petticoat hovering above her slipper clad feet.

There was nothing about her that said she was alive, but I'd been fooled too many times to take a chance. Not only that, but she was like the serpent in the Bible my ma used to tell stories about. She was evil as she was resilient.

I took a step closer.

"She's dead, sonny."

My gaze flicked up toward the center of town. Just like any gun battle there were periods of shooting and periods of silence. Men were either reloading or assessing the situation.

I started toward the action. When the heel of my boot was within a foot of Liling's body, her hand snaked out. I was ready.

I shot her in the forehead. Her expression never changed. I wanted to say, "I hope you rot in hell," but of course I didn't. Instead, I used another bullet and shot her in the neck.

Then I went to help my Uncle Turtle tidy up the mess left in Liling's wake.

Chapter 13

More Bad News

"Down, Maxwell!"

I obeyed instantly. First, because doin' so made a man a smaller target. Secondly, because Will's voice told me to do it.

As I hit the ground and spun behind a trough, a bullet caught the toe of my boot.

What on earth was Will doin' here? He was no good with a gun, and far as I knew, pretty women and gold weren't jumping out of the doorways of this little town.

Once I untied my bandana, I flung one end of it up in the air.

Immediately, bullets zinged all around me, one of 'em even puttin' a hole in the trough. Lucky it was low; otherwise, I'd be getting a bath right about now.

I heard a man scream and knew someone from Deadwood must've taken the opportunity to pick off one of the men who'd taken my bait.

The bad thing about walking into the middle of a fray was you didn't know who was who. There might be 30 men might be milling about. Of those 30, 29 of 'em might be your friend, or 29 might be your enemy.

I wondered how Ambrose and Raoul were gonna let Uncle Turtle know they were on our side. They had their work cut out, but so did I. At least one man was focusing all his attention on me, and no one liked to be pinned down, least of all me.

Another problem was me not bein' able to stop thinkin' about Huàn. I had to clear my head quick, or I wasn't gonna be doin' any thinking at all.

"Liling's dead!" I called out.

Silence followed. I was sure it meant a different thing to each man, but I truly believed that deep down, everyone felt a sense of relief.

I hoped it meant that Sheriff Benedict would put his hands up right now, but men like him usually didn't. Pride was a powerful thing in its right place, but a tad too much usually led to one's downfall.

"Who killed her?" a man yelled. It was Sheriff Benedict.

"I killed the bitch!" Maude called out in a loud but wobbly voice.

"Git down!" I ordered. She was gonna get herself killed.

She started walking toward the center of town. If she continued, she was gonna take a bullet. But I suspected that was what she wanted.

"No, Ma!" I said. We both knew she wasn't my ma, but it stopped her dead in her tracks. When she looked down at me, her watery eyes softened and her whole face transformed. I could picture her as a mother to her children, trying to do right by them. She had her peccadilloes, but we all did.

I heard the click and jumped up to get between me and whoever was gonna fire that bullet at Maude, but even as I did it, I knew I was gonna be too late.

The shot was an ear-splitting sound in the temporary quiet of the gun battle. As I spun while bringing up my gun, I saw a man standing alongside a pole that supported a roof overhang. His weapon was still pointed at us. I fired and got him.

Maude made a little *ooph* when his bullet got her, but didn't scream like most women would have. It made me think all over again that Maude was just plain tired of breathin', especially now that she didn't have any kin left.

I saw Sarge burst through a doorway and look right at me, and while it sure was good to see him, it was a mistake. There were two men on the roof across the street, picking their way along the steep grade like wobbly-kneed mountain goats. They were on the lookout for targets like Sarge.

Maude's body hit the ground with a dull thud. And while I wished I could've softened her fall and thanked her for what she did for me, doin' so would surely cause the end of me too. I had some peace of mind, though, knowing she was gonna expire near Reggie.

The two men on the roof were already getting a bead on Sarge. Oddly, it looked like my old friend had only one thought: to get my attention.

Why on earth would he do something so foolhardy? I wondered. He wasn't as clever as Jaw-Long when it came to fightin', but he'd been in the war. He knew you didn't go lookin' for trouble.

I had yet to see Ambrose, Raoul, or my Uncle Turtle. Will, either, though I'd heard his voice. And then, as if reading my mind, I saw Will shoot out from between two buildings and pluck off the two men on the roof before I could squeeze the trigger of my own weapon.

What in blazes was goin on?! I wondered. If I hadn't seen it with my own eyes, I wouldn't have believed it. Will was shootin' like a gunslinger!

But while he was taking care of the men on the rooftop, other men took the opportunity to switch positions. I saw my uncle, shootin' across the street to get closer to Sarge. Bullets *zing-pop-pup-pupped!* at his feet as he ran.

As the two men on the roof fell off and landed in the dirt, I saw a flicker of movement alongside a prancing horse. It was Sheriff Benedict.

"Hands up, Benedict!" My uncle's voice was as commanding as I remembered.

"You're in my town!" the sheriff called back.

"You're holding my nephew illegally."

A couple more shots rang out, but they were mostly wild shots. They came from farther down the street.

"Does it look like I'm holding him?"

"Only because he escaped!" This time it was Raoul.

"Stay out of this, Drake!"

The word, Drake, threw me for a loop, but mainly because I hadn't given any thought to what Raoul's surname was. I knew it wasn't gonna be the same as mine, but Drake sounded more English than French, and he told me once that he was French. .

"Your wife was a murderer, sheriff," Raoul continued.

I was glad he was speaking, because my uncle, Will, and Sarge would know not to shoot him.

"Liling had nothing to do with any of Maxwell Beck's criminal activities," Benedict volleyed back.

"Maxwell Beck is not a criminal!" Will yelled in a surprisingly sure voice.

"Not what the posters say," Sheriff Benedict argued.

"My nephew's name was cleared months ago." It was my uncle this time, and I could tell by the hard edge to his voice he was through playing games.

"Then take your nephew and git!"

As I listened to the two sheriffs' exchange, I took a gander to see if there were any possible threats to my uncle and Sarge. Then, just as I saw a man bring his gun out from behind a beam, I heard a gunshot and the man fell to the boardwalk. It was Will shootin' again!

"Surrender your weapon, Sheriff Benedict! That goes for whoever else is siding with you," my uncle said.

"Don't shoot!" said one man, taking tentative steps toward the middle of the dusty street.

It was Wilfred, the deputy I'd tussled with. He didn't have

much choice except to surrender, but he was putting himself in harm's way by doin' so.

I glanced at the sheriff. He had to be one unhappy man right about now, and I was right. When he came out shootin' a second later, he took a hail of bullets. Unfortunately, not all the shots he fired were random. One of 'em found Sarge. And judging from the way the old cook fell, the bullet was gonna end his life too.

Not surprisingly, the rest of Sheriff Benedict's men slunk off like kicked cats. I was glad. I'd witnessed enough killing to last a lifetime.

My Uncle Turtle knelt down at Sarge's side while Will came out from where he'd been pickin' off bad guys. Raoul and Ambrose stepped out too. I walked over to Sarge and knelt at his side. After I said a prayer much like I had for ma and pa, I got to my feet.

"I'll be right back," I told my uncle and Will. I wasn't gonna rest easy 'til I knew Liling was dead this time.

As I neared Liling's still body, I heard an angelic sounding voice:

"Sonny."

My glance went to Maude. Though I was sure she was dead when I left her, I saw one of her fingers twitch. She was alive! I picked her head up off the road and cradled it in the crook of my arm.

"Maude? Can you hear me? I'm gonna git you some help," I told her in what I hoped was a comforting tone of voice.

Her eyes stayed shut, but I bent my ear close to her mouth in case she had something more to say.

"Your girl."

My heart skipped a beat. She meant Patience, but she was silent for so long after she said those two words that I truly thought she'd perished. Then I heard a faint gasp of air go into her lungs.

"San. Fran." She paused. "Cisco."

Patience was in San Francisco.

"Thank you, Maude," I said. The old woman could've just died easy, but she stayed alive so she could tell me what I needed to know. "I'll never forget your kindness."

Her fingers clutched the fabric of my trousers near my shinbone. "Reggie," she said, and the word was clear as a bell. She even had a smile on her face. She wanted to die touching her man.

I gathered her body in my arms and carried her the few steps to where Reggie lay in the dirt, flies already buzzing around his dead body.

As gently as I could, I placed her alongside him. Her smile never faded. Then her fingers began to tremble. It was almost as if she were reaching out to take Reggie's hand on the way to meet their Maker.

As I moved her hand inside his, all the air in her lungs seemed to leave her, though her smile stayed put.

Troubling as it was, I forced myself look at Huàn lyin' still in the dirt not far from Reggie and Maude. The sight of all the blood pooled around his neck and chest made my guts clench. He was dead because of me.

I don't know what made me look toward the end of the road, but I was glad I did. Hinto, on his trusty paint, slowly raised his hand. Then he turned his horse around and headed west.

He made me realize I'd lost a lot, but I hadn't lost everything.

 The Clean Up

My uncle was still kneeling at Sarge's side when I returned, but got to his feet when he saw me. "He didn't have long, son. Remitting fever had a death grip on him."

Sarge was always grumping about his "battle scars" but I thought they were the outside kind, not something working on him from the inside out.

"It was his last wish," Uncle Turtle said, then stopped and swallowed hard before continuing. "To see you one last time, Maxwell." He smiled then. "He got his wish. He died a happy man."

"I sure am gonna miss seein' him scratch his belly," I said, and Uncle Turtle grinned along with me. "That and eating his molasses beans. They sure were tasty."

We both looked down at our friend. Except for the blood on his shirt, he could've been taking a nap. Even his usually wild hair looked tame. He looked as peaceful as I'd ever seen him, even napping in the bunkhouse.

The year that had come and gone since I'd seen Turtle had changed both of us. Standing next to my uncle, I realized I was now taller than he was. I noticed, too, that he had a fair amount of silver threaded through his hair and mustache. I sure hoped it wasn't from him trying to get my name cleared. Beyond the gray hair, though, there was weariness about him. I hoped things would be good for him again, once he got this business behind him...

Will joined us. This time I noticed he was wearing a badge.

"That was some fancy shootin', Will. For a minute, I thought you had a twin."

"Wiseacre," he said with a grin. "Good to see you, brother. I missed you." He shook my hand and stared at me for a long moment, then gave me one of his shoulder punches.

The pleasure at seein' each other didn't last long. We all had things we needed to attend to before we could move forward.

"Guess I'm gonna have to buy a wagon," Turtle said. "Gotta get Sarge home so I can bury him on the ranch." He faced me then. "It's a shame about Huàn."

I hoped there'd be a time when I'd be able to talk freely about Huàn without getting choked up, but it wasn't now. I cleared my throat and looked down the street to where Ambrose and Raoul were talking.

"Sarge said he wanted you to have his horse in the event he didn't make it," Uncle Turtle told me. "Jaw-Long trained him. He has potential, but he's no Huàn. Answers to the name of Hoss."

I was sure gonna miss Sarge. I turned my glance where Maude, Reggie, and Huàn lay dead in the sun. So many good beings dead for no good reason at all. And then I looked at Liling. I wished I could say I felt happy she was finally dead, but I didn't. I wasn't sure what I felt.

"I'm the one who killed Liling," I said.

Will blinked a couple of times, but he didn't seem as torn up about it as I thought he might.

"She was an evil woman, Maxwell. Jaw-Long ain't gonna hold it against you," Uncle Turtle said.

"I'll see about a wagon," Will said. "You can catch Maxwell up on things back home." He looked toward Liling's body. "When I get back, I'll help bury the ones who're staying."

Will headed down the street. I saw that the Dragon Saloon was opposite of the undertaker's shop. The saloon would be my last stop before I headed out of town; I still had questions for Raoul. But first, I had one for my uncle.

"How'd you know I was here? Raoul?"

My uncle nodded. "My biggest worry was that we weren't gonna get here in time." He clapped a hand on my shoulder. "Glad you're in one piece."

"Thank you, sir. For clearing my name, too."

"It took me a lot longer to sort through the snarl of lies Liling left in her wake than I figured it would. I finally had to enlist the help of President Cleveland."

His words stunned me. "You've done more for me than any human being 'cept Ma and Pa. I don't know that I'll ever be able to repay you."

He looked touched. "Just keep staying out from behind bullets."

"Is Miss Cordelia well?"

He smiled then, and I could tell his feelings for his wife had only deepened. I was glad he found the woman he was meant to be with. "Hasn't been a day that she hasn't talked about you." He paused. "Or said a prayer for you."

"Please tell her I said they're appreciated, and that I miss her."

Uncle Turtle's expression sobered. "You know about Patience leaving."

I nodded, though the word, *leaving,* gave me pause. My uncle made it sound as if Patience decided to take off for parts unknown all on her own. "When?"

"A few days after Will returned home. Almost a year now. Ben and Katharine have withered without her."

My heart sank. "Why'd she leave?"

"Maude Reggie came for her. She was sent by Patience's pa."

Maude Reggie had to be the Maude, who was lying dead in the dirt alongside her man, Reggie. My brain strove to make sense of the nonsensical situation.

"Where'd they go?"

"Alaska."

"I don't believe so."

The look on my uncle's face said he was taken aback. "What makes you say that?"

"The woman and man close to Huàn – that's Maude and Reggie. Liling made 'em do some pretty bad things. I'm guessing that's one of 'em."

Uncle Turtle's face said he was still having a hard time figuring out what was goin' on.

"Before Maude expired, she told me Patience was in San Francisco." At my uncle's deepening frown, I continued. "I think Maude got Patience away from Deadwood, then handed her over to someone who took her to San Francisco."

That's as far as I wanted to think. If I imaged what happened after that, I wasn't sure I'd be able to function.

"I believe Patience needs me," I said. I didn't want to elaborate about the picture of Patience that Liling had given to Ambrose.

He uttered a mirthless laugh, then ran his fingers down his long mustache. "Jaw-Long is gonna die long before he gets a chance to right all of Liling's wrongs."

"I'm goin' to San Francisco."

He rubbed his forehead. He usually did so when he was agitated. "I thought you might say that. You know I wish you well, but there's a possibility that Patience won't be..."

I sighed. "I know. That's why I need to get to her as quick as I can."

He looked like he wanted to say more, but decided better of it.

"I'm always gonna care for her. No matter what," I said.

The sight of Will hurrying back toward us ended our conversation. I was glad; the more I talked about Patience's troubles, the more troubled I became.

"The livery owner will deliver a wagon and team as soon as he's able, and the undertaker will be here shortly, too," he told Uncle Turtle.

He nodded. "You're staying?"

"Until the U. S. Deputy Marshal relieves me of my duties."

"You amaze me, Will."

"Why can't a pretty girl say those words to me?" he asked.

I grinned and shook my head. Seein' him again made me realize how much I missed talking with him. But my mood once again sobered when I thought about all I had to do before I left for San Francisco.

"I need to speak to the undertaker too, to see if I can have Maude and Reggie buried in the cemetery," I said. "I hope he'll let me make payments. They deserve to have a nice place to rest after all the traveling they've done."

"Payments?" Will asked. He and my uncle exchanged glances. "If you wish to have your two friends buried, all you need to do is let me know the amount and I'll take care of it."

What was he gettin' at? "I couldn't have you pay for it, Will," I said. "They're my friends."

"I wouldn't be paying for their burial with my funds, little brother. You'd be paying for it with yours."

When I frowned, he said, "I invested the money you gave me to hold for you, and made the same investments for myself. Gold and gold mining stocks. You and I are men of means now."

#

Chapter 15

I would've never believed it, mainly because I never gave it much thought 'til now, but money did make things easier. The undertaker even said he'd bury Huàn next to Maude and Reggie if I was willing to pay for two plots for because of his size. I liked the thought of all three of 'em being together, so I gladly agreed.

I thought I might blubber a little, but I felt so dead inside, I don't think I could've worked up tears if you paid me. Images of Huàn's beautiful, strange markings, and all the happy times we had together kept goin' through my head.

I remembered how I used to call him Juan at the beginning and how he used to try to throw me just for the pure fun of it. Later, as he got to know and like me, Huàn showed me what a true friend he was by doing all I asked of him and more.

"He sure could be bossy," I said, though I meant it kindly.

"Kicked me once," my uncle said with a grin. "Hip got a bruise the size of a melon. I thought it was gonna cripple me."

"I sure miss him," I said.

Then we turned around and walked back to town. I put my saddle in the wagon alongside Sarge. Uncle Turtle said he'd keep it for me until he returned. Then he took me to meet Hoss. I was a bit surprised Sarge managed to stay in the saddle; Hoss was a real handful.

Uncle Turtle said animals had a way of knowing when a human wasn't well. Hoss behaved himself when Sarge rode him, but with anyone else, he wasn't so compliant. Hoss sounded a lot like Huàn in that he had spirit to spare. I knew Sarge had me in mind when he chose Hoss, but I truly didn't have the time or the inclination to start fresh with another spirited horse.

"I'm gonna take the train West," I told my uncle. "It'll be faster."

I glanced to the west and suddenly remembered how me and Pa and Ma used to talk about what we were gonna do when we got to the ocean.

Pa always got dreamy-eyed at the mention of the ocean. He'd grin and say he was gonna buy a boat and scoop fish out of the ocean with his bare hands so we could feast on sea critters every day of the week if we wanted. Ma said that when we got there, she was gonna take off her shoes and walk straight into the ocean up to her neck, and let the warm waves bob her body around like a cork. Neither of 'em ever realized their dreams.

I never said it out loud, but I always wanted to take a trip across the ocean to an exotic land. But now I realized I didn't much care to go if it wasn't with Patience. I decided to run the idea by her after I found her.

"Sounds like a fine idea," my uncle said, jolting me out of my daydream.

My uncle paid for a grave for Liling, though funds for that purpose could probably be extracted from Liling and Sheriff Benedict's estate. I thought it was a fine gesture, though, and I was certain Jaw-Long would appreciate it.

"Before I go, I'd like to thank you both for all you've done," I told my uncle and Will. I left it at that. I didn't want to get mushy, but I did want them to know I truly appreciated their efforts.

"Awww, c'mon little brother. You're gonna make me get

all sentimental, and I just put on a fresh bandana," he said with a hard punch to my shoulder.

It sure was good to see Will again and in such fine form to boot.

My uncle cleared his throat. "A man can never be sure where he's gonna put down roots, but if you do decide to make Deadwood your home, I purchased two plots of land on the north side of town. One for you and one for Will."

When Will smiled, I knew he already knew about it and was glad. I was, too. I hoped Patience liked Deadwood enough to want to stay there once we got back home, but I also knew it was a little premature to think that far ahead.

"It was Miss Cordelia's idea too," my uncle said a little sheepishly. "She spends half her day designing ways to keep you both close."

"There's nowhere else I'd rather be," I said. And while the words I said were true, I suddenly felt in my heart that it would be a while before I could think about settling there, or anywhere else.

"Please give my regards to Miss Cordelia, Jaw-Long, James, and Phin," I said.

"Sure will," he said.

After me and my uncle shook hands, I got cleaned up and went to the Dragon Saloon. Raoul was waiting for me at a table in the corner.

The man at the piano pounded the keys with such exuberance, I feared he might take some of them right off it. I found his style of playing a bit disconcerting but he kept a tune, so I leaned back in my chair and enjoyed it for what it was.

A beautiful young woman appeared. She had long dark hair, almond-shaped blue eyes, and bright pink lips. She looked Oriental except for the color of her eyes and her height. When she began singing along with the music the piano player was makin', it was with a robust, hypnotic voice.

Ma used to tell me and Pa stories about beautiful mermaids who sang songs to lure sailors to them. She called the music they made siren songs.

I wondered how such a pretty girl found herself in the middle of nowhere, but she looked happy enough, so I abandoned the thought because it would most likely lead me back to Patience and her situation.

Ambrose came to our table and set down two beers for me and Raoul and then left. He seemed a little distant with me, but maybe he was feeling guilty about being part of Liling's scheme.

I took a sip of my beer and was trying to figure out the words of the singer's song when Raoul leaned toward me.

"I would like to accompany you to San Francisco."

I was starting to get a little irritated with Raoul. He'd been a big help, but he just wouldn't let go of the idea that I needed his company. I thought when he mentioned it earlier in front of Will and I told him I wasn't interested, that would be the end of it. I guess I was wrong.

"Thank you for the offer, but this is one trip I truly need to take alone." I said the words in an even, pleasant voice so he wouldn't take offense.

"Ambrose supplied me with some additional information only minutes ago," he said after a lengthy pause. I saw him give the young woman a furtive glance.

"And?" I prompted when he didn't continue.

"It seems the singer I hired a week ago is more than that."

It wasn't difficult to put two and two together. She was there to make money off lonely men. But I wasn't partial to guessing games.

"Spit it out," I said.

"Her name is Nadia Rose. At least that's what she calls herself."

"Kinda like what you do with the name Drake," I said.

He smiled kindly. "Nothing sinister, I assure you. Drake is

116

our surname, our family name," he said. "You and I are descended from English royalty. I use the name professionally."

"About the girl," I said abruptly.

Raoul didn't look insulted at my blunt prompt. "I'm certain Nadia Rose isn't her real name, but girls never share those kind of details unless it's to a man she's contemplating marrying. What I do know, is that her father is Russian and Japanese. He's also a skilled empty-hand fighter."

Now that was an intriguing term, mainly because I'd never heard it before.

"He was a farmer who became an assassin, like many of the men of his town. But he didn't fight political injustice. He fought for the pleasure of killing." He paused. "Then he came to San Francisco."

Dread filled me. I wasn't afraid for me; I was afraid for my sweet Patience.

He turned his head so Nadia couldn't see his face. I didn't flick my glance over at her, but I could tell she was watching us intently as she sang.

"Nadia's father and Liling were associates. I'm certain Nadia's father accompanied Patience to San Francisco."

Though the new information wasn't surprising, I had already begun to piece things together for myself before Raoul filled in the blanks. It made an already dire situation even worse.

"So you think the girl is here to keep an eye on me?"

Before he could answer, I heard a change in the girl's voice. And by the instantaneous change in Raoul's demeanor, I knew she was on her way over to us.

As she neared our table, she continued singing in a language I didn't understand. Then, when she was between us, she placed one hand on the side of my face, and the other on Raoul's. She slowly smoothed her silky fingertips down my jaw.

I moved away from her touch on the pretense of taking

another swallow of my beer; I didn't want to be anywhere near her. As far as I was concerned, she was trouble.

"Do you feel lucky, lucky, lucky?" she began singing to me in English in that sultry voice of hers. I could see Raoul was getting a kick out of the attention she was paying me, despite his warning to me about her possible reason for being in Plankville.

I don't know why, but I started getting angry. Huàn, Sarge, Maude, and Reggie were dead. While I couldn't say I was disappointed that Liling wouldn't be causing anymore problems, a lot of good souls had died today for no good reason. And to top it off, Patience was probably in a whole heap of trouble.

"Goodbye," I told Raoul and left the saloon. If I stayed much longer, I wasn't sure what I'd do. I had more to say to Raoul, but it would keep until I made my way back to Deadwood with Patience.

Once I was outside, I took a deep breath. The air was earthy, even at this end of town, due to the lingering smell of freshly-turned earth coming from all the new graves in the cemetery. I knew I'd never sniff a freshly-turned farm field again without picturing fresh graves.

I had already said goodbye to my uncle and Raoul. Hoss was going to be boarded at the livery until I returned for him. The only thing I needed to do before I left was say my final farewell to Will.

"Stagecoach passes through tomorrow for Denver," Will said when I entered the office. "From there you need to catch the Pacific Coast Express to Salt Lake City. From Salt Lake City, it'll be the Pacific Railroad to San Francisco." He had a sheaf of paperwork in front of him. He truly looked like he was born a lawman.

"Much obliged for all you've done. I still feel a bit boggled at the changes you've been through." I smiled so he wouldn't think I meant any bad by my words. "Please don't tell me you've given up on the ladies."

"Not quite," he told me, a charming smile coming to his face. "Though I truly am thinking of choosing one and settling down. Mother said she'd like to live to see grandchildren."

I smiled then because it wasn't hard to picture her saying those very words.

The door of the sheriff's office opened and Raoul walked in. He had a strange look on his face.

"I wasn't finished talkin' with you."

"I figured I'd stop and see you on my way back through," I told him. I wasn't about to stay at the saloon and get touched by a woman who was most likely up to no good.

"No. It's not that," he said, looking at me like I was a daft child.

"What then?" I said, then nodded toward Will. "You can speak freely. I don't have any secrets from him or you."

He gave Will a look and nodded. "A young girl came to the saloon with a baby."

I didn't see what that had to do with anything. It was a little unorthodox, but I would've thought stranger things than that happened in a town like Plankville.

"The girl was looking for Nadia."

Raoul was beginning to get on my nerves. Why was he having such trouble with words all of a sudden?

"This Nadia – is she the baby's mother?" Will asked, saving me the trouble.

Raoul shook his head and his forehead scrunched up a bit. He didn't look at all like a successful businessman at that moment. He looked like a confused boy.

"The baby is Liling's."

Neither me nor Will said a word. I was so stunned, I don't think you coulda dragged a single syllable out me with a team of horses. It took me a few seconds to accept what I was hearing before I was able to ask:

"Did you know about the baby?"

Raoul shook his head. He was telling the truth. Will's face went white. I don't know why. It wasn't like he was the father. Was he?

"Will?" I asked.

"What?" He frowned. "You don't think I had anything to do with her having a baby, do you?"

"Just askin'." I turned to Raoul then. "How old is it?"

"A month or two. I don't know all that much about babies. Children were Liling's specialty," Raoul said.

That much was true. As big of a tyrant as she was, she had a soft spot for children. I suppose it wasn't that much of a stretch to picture her wanting one of her own. But then I thought about what Maude and Reggie said about Liling ending their young daughter's life, and I began to have my doubts.

"Now that both she and Sheriff Benedict are dead, I guess the child is an orphan." Will paused and looked at me. "Unless Jaw-Long wants to assume the care of the child."

I couldn't picture him not doing so. Honor coursed through Jaw-Long's veins. And even though Liling had dishonored him, he would probably think of raising the baby to live an exceptionally honorable life as a way to make up for all the trouble Liling had caused.

"Nadia said she's taking the baby to San Francisco."

"Why on earth would she do that?" I was taken aback by the brazenness of the stranger's intentions.

"She said she will take the baby to its father."

"You believe this woman?" Will asked.

"She works at my saloon and keeps to herself when she's not entertaining guests," Raoul said, which didn't answer his question.

I only had a few minutes in Nadia's presence and I had

120

my doubts that she could be trusted.

"Max?"

"It's none of my beeswax," I said with a shrug. "I suppose it's something for the law to figure out.

In another time and place, I might have found the entire conversation a little humorous; here we were, three men talking about a baby like a gaggle of church ladies. Today I didn't have a bit of humor left in me.

"I'm going to speak with her and advise her that the baby must remain in Plankville until all legal avenues have been explored.

"You sound like you've been on the job for ten years," I said, still amazed by the change in Will. A year ago, some of the men on the ranch had even called him a lay about. Now he was taking action like some Philadelphia lawyer with a case to prove.

"Your uncle was adamant that I learn how to protect my mother and the ranch in case he wasn't able. I began learning the law too. The shootin' part evolved naturally."

I didn't see nothin' natural about learnin' how to shoot. One had to really want to learn the skill. Or need to learn it. Shootin' wasn't something that grew on you like learnin' to strum the guitar.

"Something happened," I said.

Will shook his head. Out of the corner of my eye, I saw Raoul narrow his eyes.

"Someone nearly took Jaw-Long's life. In the bunkhouse, no less."

I was flabbergasted. Jaw-Long's fighting skills were so good they were almost beyond what I thought was humanly possible. As far as I was concerned, he was invincible.

"Who?"

"Still don't know his name, but the sheriff and Phin managed to put a couple of bullets in him before he disappeared. He was a big Chinaman."

Things were getting stranger by the minute. "Why would anyone want to kill Jaw-Long?" I said out loud, but what I really meant was, *Who else besides Liling would want to hurt him?*

Will shrugged.

"I think it would be best if I accompanied you to San Francisco," Raoul said.

"What a fine idea!" Will said before I could open my mouth.

"I don't need anyone to accompany me," I told Raoul.

He suddenly smiled. "We're all well aware of that you don't need any company. I was just thinking we might get to know each other better."

While he appeared sincere, there was a little part of me that couldn't help but think he wanted to be there for Patience if things didn't work out between me and her.

"If it were me, I'd be glad of the chance to travel with someone I knew," Will said, his eyes bright.

"Not much for conversation," I said, hoping my words sounded less stern than they sounded to my ears. "But I will stop by on my way back through. You have my word." I faced Will. "Please tell everyone that I'll be home with Patience before they know it."

"You better, Maxwell. Otherwise, I'm gonna start spending your money," Will joked.

"You have my permission," I said, then left the sheriff's office.

On my way to the cemetery, I spotted the young boy I'd seen when I first came to town. He was running among the graves now. He saw me, then abruptly turned and raced toward Huàn's grave. Once he was atop it, he kicked up a clump of dirty earth with his shoes. The gesture irritated me more than it should have.

"This is a place of respect," I told him. "How'd you like it if someone walked across your dead body?"

He looked up at me with his grimy face for a long moment. Just when I thought he was gonna run away with his tail between his legs or say he was sorry, he stuck his tongue out at me.

I wasn't used to dealin' with children, so his doin' something so purely naughty took me off guard. Before I could think of a thing to say in rebuttal, he ran away like he had a swarm of bees chasin' him.

I watched the little imp until he was out of sight and then turned back around. My stomach twisted at the thought of my dear friend Huàn, lying dead beneath a pile of dirt, never again able to come running when I whistled, or rub his face against mine.

Once I regained my composure, I closed my eyes for a brief second and said a prayer for Huàn, Maude, and Reggie.

I bypassed the main street and went to livery to give Hoss another look. I figured if he didn't work out for me, I'd give him to Patience. While there I realized I'd already spent more time in that town than I wanted, so I purchased an ordinary riding horse with the intentions of selling him when I reached Denver, then quietly rode out of town.

As I put Plankville behind me, I couldn't help but feel that the strange silence that accompanied me might be a harbinger of even worse danger ahead.

Chapter 16

Derailed

About ten miles into my ride northwest, I met up with Hinto. He was alone again, and I wasn't surprised to see him.

He stayed with me for a day's ride. We stopped for the night in a grassy, rolling area and set up camp. My gut told me it would be the last time I'd see him for a long while. I thought he might say something about Huàn, but he didn't.

We ate a rabbit he killed and as we were lookin' into the pretty, crackling' flames of our campfire, he said, quite out of the blue:

"I dream about you last night."

My ears perked up. He must've thought it was pretty important to mention it.

"You go west. To big water," he said, slowly moving his arms out around him.

I nodded.

"Bad men look for you," he said in that fine, halting way of his. "Find girl with gold hair. You make bad medicine."

Those last three words sure gave me pause. As patiently as I could, I waited for more.

He gave me a long, unblinking look. "If a man would do great things, he would not do them alone."

Hinto had trained me in a number of things, but each of them was more or less solitary pursuits that were designed to keep me breathing. I had a feeling he was talking about that dream of his. Was he talking about Patience? Or something more sinister?

I pulled the photo of Patience out of my vest pocket and handed it to him. He glanced at it and then put it into the flames. I was shocked he would do such a thing, and maybe even a little angry until he spoke.

"Do not be afraid to cry. It will free your mind."

While Hinto usually only said things that needed saying, he rarely said anything sentimental. I knew he only had my best interests at heart, so I nodded and watched the image of Patience curl, then blacken in the licking flames until it was so much ash.

A thin plume of acrid smoke rose at the end, and bits of black ash fluttered into the sky. One little bit of it landed on my face. I didn't brush it off. While I wasn't superstitious by nature, I knew it would leave me with a bad feeling if I were to wipe it off.

And that was the end. Hinto was done talkin'.

We spent a companionable spell around the fire, then I turned in. When I woke up, I wrapped a few coins in a bandana and handed them to Hinto. While it was obvious he didn't expect the gesture, he graciously accepted my gift and handed me a short knife in a hand-beaded pouch. It had been used much and it meant all the more to me.

I headed northwest on the crowbait I bought in Plankville. I had to force myself not to ride him hard. From the moment me and Hinto parted ways, something began to push me to move faster. It was almost as if Patience was whispering in my ear, "Where are you, Maxwell? I can't wait much longer."

When I reached Denver, I sold the horse, purchased a first class ticket and rode in surprising luxury to Salt Lake City where I purchased another ticket for the final leg of my journey.

Uncle Turtle said I had a fascination with trains that wasn't normal for a cowboy. It was amazing to me how the caterpillar-like machine with so many separate components could move along as one perfect machine. So when I had the chance, I spoke with conductors and engineers. Each had wild stories to tell about robbers, derailments, and other such incidents. Advances in tools and equipment were coming in leaps and bounds too. I would be riding to the West Coast in a car that was fitted with Janney, knuckle style, couplers, a big improvement over the link and pin couplers typically used on freight trains.

A brakesman told me a little about how things worked when he caught me looking at a car near the front of the train. I suppose he liked having people think he had an important job. I did notice he was missing his pinky finger on his right hand down to the first knuckle joint. It made me wonder how such a thing would affect my aim.

We talked for a bit and when I told him my name, he blinked a couple times.

"Maxwell Beck. Son of the sheriff of Deadwood?"

I was never sure what kind of reception an admission was gonna get me, but he had a kindly face, so I nodded, even though I wasn't Uncle Turtle's son by birth. I guess people really didn't give a hoot if I was his son or his nephew. They just liked the stories they heard about me, though some of 'em didn't have much truth in 'em.

The thing that surprised me most was that he was asking me who I was related to in Deadwood, when we were in Salt Lake City, miles and miles from Deadwood.

"Wait 'til I tell the engineer we got a celebrity on board."

"I'd rather you didn't. I'm just a cowboy," I said. "Not much for attention."

"It really is you." He stuck out his hand. "Name's Hank Butterfield."

After I shook his hand, he motioned for me to stay where I was. "I'll be just a minute."

While he was gone, I got down on my hands and knees

126

and looked at the underside of the car. Everything was pretty straight forward with no surprises. When Hank came back a moment later, he was wearing a wide smile.

"If it's all right with you, Ike Patterson, the engineer, would like to speak with you this evening in the club car after dinner."

"It would be an honor."

He gave a surreptitious glance to the area around us, as if to make sure no one was trying to overhear our conversation. "We've been having some difficulties with attempted robberies. We do have a detective and a lawman on board, but..."

"You can count on me."

Hank grinned and clapped me on the shoulder. This particular train was billed as a passenger train, and robberies were becoming rare, although I guessed there was nothing from stopping the company from transporting gold along with the passengers if they so desired.

"Would you like a tour of the cars before we begin boarding?"

"Sure would," I said. Not only was I curious, it was good to know the lay of the train, should I need to get from one place to another in a hurry.

"I'll tell the porter who you are, but also to keep the information to himself."

We went from car to car. They were surprisingly luxurious. It was like touring a rich man's house on wheels. I took note of how the doors opened and closed and how many windows there were and the purpose of each car. I didn't get to go to the engine car because it was almost time for the passengers to start boarding.

I took a seat, kept my head low and started reading the paper I brought with me. It had been a while since I'd been in the midst of such a large group of people. I heard small children, old ladies, and gents. I smelled perfume that remind me of Patience, cigar smoke, and even horsehair, as if one of the passengers had just swung from his saddle into the train.

The bell rang and I listened to the sounds of final preparation for departure as well as the passengers themselves; chatter buzzed in my ears from every angle.

One common topic was the fine Mormon building said to house the tabernacle. I wouldn't have minded taking a gander at it myself, but I heard that if you weren't a Mormon, you couldn't enter. Most of the conversation, however, centered on what was on the menu for the evening in the dining car.

A young couple sat next me. They seemed wrapped up in each other, but did manage to tear their gazes away long enough to take note of me. They sent a kind smile my way and immediately began conversing again in soft, loving tones.

Without being obvious, I took in all the passengers ahead of me, and to the side of me. The porter gave me an extra long look and a nod on the way past, but I didn't acknowledge it. Outlaws were always on the lookout for clues about who was who on the train.

Once we pulled away from the station, I decided to stretch my legs and take in the rest of passengers behind me. I wasn't paranoid by nature, but I preferred feelin' comfortable over uncertain.

As I stood up, I immediately heard a sound that made me pause.

A-wah. A-wah-wah. A-wah!

It was a baby. I truly hadn't been around a lot of babies in my lifetime, but I'd recognize the sound of a fairly fresh baby nywhere.

Even before I turned around, I had a feeling I wasn't like what I saw. Turned out I was only partially wrong.

e rear of the car, I spotted a man, woman, and baby her. The woman was trying to comfort the new-born, but she looked dern uncomfortable doing it. Part of the reason could've been because she wasn't the baby's mother.

But even more startling than seeing Nadia with a baby in her arms was seein' the man sittin' next to her. Raoul looked even more ill at ease than Nadia did.

Either he caught sight of me out of the corner of his eye, or Nadia somehow alerted him to the fact that I was in front of him, because he abruptly looked in my direction.

Just as abruptly, he looked back down at the baby. Then he leisurely brought his hand to his head. When he ran his fingers through his hair, he crooked one finger away from his skull so that it was facing the window to his other side.

He was telling me there was something I needed to take note of.

I switched my glance to the window he indicated and felt my stomach sink.

Raoul wasn't trying to get me to take note of something.

He was trying to get me to take note of *someone*.

The End

Thanks for joining Max on yet another adventure. I hope you'll ride along with him as he searches for Patience in Book 4.

S. A. Ferkey